PRAISE FOR
All God's Sparrows and Other Stories

"*All God's Sparrows* is a captivating work of fiction surrounding the life of Mary Fields, which humanizes a much-maligned and stereotyped Western figure. Leslie Budewitz's Mary Fields is sensitive, intuitive, and remarkably understanding of the people around her, who in turn show her respect and deference borne of the considerable skills she acquired on the Montana frontier. Budewitz captures a complex and complicated Mary Fields and comes closer to the truth than the caricatures that have evolved around the remarkable life of this singular woman of the West."
—Quintard Taylor, PhD.,
Founder of BlackPast.org

"Finely researched and richly detailed, *All God's Sparrows and Other Stories* is a wonderful collection. I loved learning about this fascinating woman . . . and what a character she is! Kudos to Leslie Budewitz for bringing her to life so vividly."
—Kathleen Grissom, *New York Times*
bestselling author of *Crow Mary*

"In *All God's Sparrows and Other Stories: A Stagecoach Mary Fields Collection*, Leslie Budewitz masterfully illuminates the life of 'Stagecoach Mary' Fields with a deft hand and empathetic eye. Skillfully blending fact and fiction, Budewitz vividly portrays the remarkable journey of this little-known woman of the West, shining a light on her courage, resilience, and unyielding commitment to justice. Budewitz's exceptional storytelling prowess is evident throughout this captivating collection of short stories as Mary Fields takes her well-deserved place in the sun."

—Ann Parker, author of the award-winning Silver Rush mystery series

"In this beautifully drawn portrait of Mary Fields and life in 1897 Montana, Leslie Budewitz weaves stories of hardship and dedication, mystery and love. From a half-Blackfeet child to a forthright lady of the night to active and former missionary nuns, you'll read rich studies of human hearts, the tough life of the frontier, and the contemplative mind of Stagecoach Mary, a formerly enslaved woman who finds her own place in the West bringing justice for the less powerful. *All God's Sparrows and Other Stories* is a must-read by a master writer."

—Edith Maxwell/Maddie Day, Agatha Award-winning author of the historical Quaker Midwife Mysteries and *A Case for the Ladies: A Dot and Amelia Mystery*

"Impeccably researched and written with clear fondness and respect for the once-living people who inspire the characters of *All God's Sparrows and Other Stories*, Leslie Budewitz has crafted fiction that demystifies the American West while honoring the strength of individual spirit that resides as the region's most enduring characteristic. Set in the final years of the Montana Territory and the early decades of statehood, Budewitz breathes life into her protagonist, Mary Fields, a real-life former slave who became a fixture in the high plains town of Cascade, Montana. Centering these stories on the novel point of view offered by Fields is smart and fulfilling, and Mary's access to the people living in this sparse, enchanting landscape through her position as its mail carrier offers intimate knowledge of her neighbors' lives, feeding our

fascination with the history unearthed and the small mysteries that propel these stories. Budewitz has created a rich, fully fleshed constellation of characters with a star at their center in Mary that will leave readers hoping that she will write a second volume."
—Mark Hummel, author of *Man, Underground* and *In the Chameleon's Shadow*

"A suspenseful and riveting story cycle. Budewitz expertly balances established historical detail with a storyteller's sense of possibility—and an uplifting compassion, too."
—Art Taylor, Edgar Award-winning author of *The Adventures of the Castle Thief and Other Expeditions and Indiscretions*

"Mary Fields, or 'Stagecoach Mary,' was the first African American woman to serve as a U.S. mail carrier. She was known to smoke cigars, tote a rifle while packing hidden pistols, and wear long black skirts like the Ursuline sisters she nursed, fed, and worked alongside as they struggled to establish a school for Blackfeet girls at St. Peter's Mission in Montana Territory. Leslie Budewitz pens a lyrical tribute to this tireless caretaker of all those infirm, young, fragile, or helpless. When told she 'shall be blest in heaven,' Mary's response is pitch-perfect: 'Mary grunted. "The Bible says God watches over the sparrows. But I figure even He can use a little help from time to time."' I love Budewitz's portrayal of this iconic hero as motherly and bold as the West was wide. Even God needs her. As do we."
—Sidney Thompson, author of *The Bass Reeves Trilogy*

BOOKS BY LESLIE BUDEWITZ

*All God's Sparrows and Other Stories:
A Stagecoach Mary Fields Collection*

Food Lovers' Village Mysteries

Death al Dente
Crime Rib
Butter Off Dead
Treble at the Jam Fest
As the Christmas Cookie Crumbles
Carried to the Grave and Other Stories

Spice Shop Mysteries

Assault and Pepper
Guilty as Cinnamon
Killing Thyme
Chai Another Day
The Solace of Bay Leaves
Peppermint Barked
Between a Wok and a Dead Place
To Err is Cumin

Destination Murders Short Story Series (Contributor)

"The Picture of Guilt: A Food Lovers' Village Short Story"
(in *Murder in the Mountains*)
"Seafood Rub: A Spice Shop Short Story" (in *Murder at Sea*)

MORE BOOKS BY LESLIE BUDEWITZ

Nonfiction and Cookbooks

Books, Crooks and Counselors: How to Write Accurately About Criminal Law and Courtroom Procedure

Contributor

The Cozy Cookbook: More than 100 Recipes from Today's Bestselling Mystery Authors
The Mystery Writers of America Cookbook
Writes of Passage: Adventures on the Writer's Journey
How to Write a Mystery: A Handbook by Mystery Writers of America
Promophobia: Taking the Mystery Out of Promoting Crime Fiction

Writing as Alicia Beckman

Bitterroot Lake
Blind Faith

ALL GOD'S SPARROWS
AND
OTHER STORIES

A STAGECOACH MARY FIELDS COLLECTION

LESLIE BUDEWITZ

All God's Sparrows and Other Stories
Beyond the Page Books
are published by
Beyond the Page Publishing
www.beyondthepagepub.com

Copyright © 2024 by Leslie Ann Budewitz.
Three of these stories originally appeared in a slightly different form in *Alfred Hitchcock Mystery Magazine*: "All God's Sparrows: A Stagecoach Mary Story," *Alfred Hitchcock Mystery Magazine* (May/June 2018), copyright © 2018 Leslie Ann Budewitz; "Miss Starr's Goodbye: A Stagecoach Mary Story," *Alfred Hitchcock Mystery Magazine* (Nov/Dec 2019), copyright © 2019 Leslie Ann Budewitz; and "Coming Clean: A Stagecoach Mary Story," *Alfred Hitchcock Mystery Magazine* (Jan/Feb 2021), copyright © 2021 Leslie Ann Budewitz.
Cover design and illustration by Dar Albert, Wicked Smart Designs

ISBN: 978-1-960511-74-4

All rights reserved under International and Pan-American Copyright Conventions. By payment of required fees, you have been granted the non-exclusive, non-transferable right to access and read the text of this book. No part of this text may be reproduced, transmitted, downloaded, decompiled, reverse engineered, or stored in or introduced into any information storage and retrieval system, in any form or by any means, whether electronic or mechanical, now known or hereinafter invented without the express written permission of both the copyright holder and the publisher.

This is a work of fiction. Names, characters, places, and incidents either are the product of the author's imagination or are used fictitiously, and any resemblance to actual persons, living or dead, business establishments, events or locales is entirely coincidental. The publisher does not have any control over and does not assume any responsibility for author or third-party websites or their content.

The scanning, uploading, and distribution of this book via the Internet or via any other means without the permission of the publisher is illegal and punishable by law. Your support of the author's rights is appreciated.

CONTENTS

All God's Sparrows	1
Miss Starr's Goodbye	18
Coming Clean	36
A Bitter Wind	56
Historical Notes	147

For those whose stories have been lost,
and those who work to keep the stories alive.

ALL GOD'S SPARROWS

At the sight of the barefoot girl, half hidden by a thicket of chokecherry, Mary called to the horses.

"Whoa, Peter. Hold up there, Paul." She tightened the reins and slowed the wagonload of timbers for the sisters' new laundry. They were sore in need after the old washhouse burned, and Mary meant to build the thing herself if she had to.

The horses stopped, the chestnut stomping in protest. A poof of fine gray-brown dirt blew into Mary's face. She sneezed, a mighty sound that knocked her straw hat loose. The chestnut flicked his ears.

Mary wiped her black shirtsleeve across her face before sizing up the girl. Nine or ten, in a blue calico dress that was clean though too short and far too tight. She cradled a reed basket of eggs against her middle.

"You're that woman they call Black Mary, aren't you?" The girl's voice was steady, her dark eyes curious.

"Mary Fields, young miss, making my rounds." Mary shifted her wide hips. The plank seat got hard after the drive to the mill near Cascade, despite the rough woolen blanket beneath her. Beside her, the black dog with the white blaze shifted, too. Had she known how badly rutted this shortcut was, she'd have stuck to the main road. "Oh, these old bones is tired."

"Do you work for the nuns? The ones who run the girls' school?"

"I do. I do whatever the sisters need—haul freight, grow potatoes and carrots—" Mary glanced at the basket in the girl's thin brown arms, and stopped herself from saying "raise chickens and kill 'em." "Boil up a mess a laundry. Them long black skirts they wear gather this dust something awful, I'll tell you."

"Do you have to know how to read to go to school?"

"No, you don't. They'll learn you to read. How old you be?"

"Nine, I think."

With those dark eyes and high cheekbones, her nearly black hair combed and braided, Mary suspected the child had Indian blood. Blackfeet, likely, in these parts. She squinted, peering through the dense shrubs, and caught sight of a weathered log cabin perched above the creek. In the brush, a sparrow whistled.

"Can your parents read and write?"

"My pa can, but he's too busy to teach me. He runs range cattle."

Meaning he was a white man. Meaning he'd be away long stretches, leaving this girl home with her mother, whom he might not have bothered to marry, if she was Blackfeet.

A rooster crowed—midday, but that figured. Seemed to her in any species, some males liked to crow whenever they damn well pleased.

"Easy, boy," she told the dog, who lowered his head.

"Josie, don't give the traveler any trouble," a woman called from behind the wild shrubs. A moment later, she came into view, dark-haired, moving slowly, thick with pregnancy.

"Ma'am," Mary said. She'd guessed right. Probably a half-breed, not much more than twenty-five. "Your girl here being kind to an old lady who mostly talks to herself."

"Josie, get the bucket and offer our visitor a drink of water."

Wordlessly, Josie set the basket of eggs at her mother's feet, then dashed down the path.

"You're Mary Fields," the woman said, her voice soft, her eyes lowered.

Mary inclined her head, questioning.

"Everyone knows you," the woman continued. "You're that Negro woman who works for the sisters at St. Peter's Mission. You saved Mother Amadeus's life when she had pneumonia."

That had been three months ago, in the spring of 1885, when Mary made the long voyage with a group of Ursuline sisters from Toledo, a pistol hidden in her skirt. First to Chicago, then by rail to St. Paul, and westward through the Dakotas into Montana Territory. The last leg, overland by wagon, brought them to St. Peter's, where, praise the Lord, she'd found Mother Amadeus weak, but alive. That good woman had said just thinking of the fit Mary would throw if she arrived only to find her dead and buried had given her the strength to live.

Mary gazed at the pregnant woman, whose brown fingers worked to ease the pain in her low back. Her eyes were pinched, and the remnants of a bruise clung to her cheekbone.

"You know my name, ma'am, but I don't know yours."

"My people call me Wawatseka." *Pretty woman.* "My husband calls me Annie."

Josie staggered into view, water sloshing from the bucket. She regained her balance, her footfalls startling the leghorn trailing her. The hen squawked, flapped its wings, and fled.

Panting heavily, the girl set the bucket down.

Annie lifted the ladle to the stranger. Mary took it in her big hands and drank it dry. Annie dipped it into the bucket a second time.

"Mama," Josie said, "it's true. They are teaching girls now. I bet they have books and desks and blackboards and everything."

No surprise that the effort to persuade Indians to send their children to school had missed this isolated road and family.

"Hush, little sparrow. You know what your pa said," Annie replied, and the girl's face fell. "That tradesman had no right to fill your head with tales."

That explained how the child had heard about schools and blackboards.

"Not that it's any business of mine," Mary said as she took the ladle again, "but Josie tells me your husband runs cattle. You got a woman to be with you when your time comes? Your mother or sister, a neighbor?" Though neighbors were scarce. Mary had seen less than a handful of occupied cabins in the dozen miles between Mission and town.

"My family's all gone." Annie ran a hand over her daughter's head, and the girl leaned against her. "Josie will do for me."

Mary had tended many pregnant women on the farm, then in the households where she'd worked after the war. She knew from the pain on Annie's face and the swelling in her hands and ankles that she was not well. With no one but a man and a child to care for her—and him no doubt useless, if he could be bothered to stay home—Mary feared for her and the babe.

She drained the ladle and handed it back, shaking her head at the offer of more. "Can you spare a few eggs? Our hens been laying poorly these last weeks—can't think why—and the sisters sure would like a fresh taste of egg in the morning." This was a lie—Mary's hens didn't dare stop laying—but she didn't figure God would mind.

Annie agreed readily and handed up the eggs. Mary wrapped a dozen in her kerchief and tucked the precious cargo in the box beneath the seat. She dug a few coins out of a small buckskin bag. At least Annie would have money for supplies. Mary would get a message to the tradesman to stop by, even if he'd been rudely sent away before.

"Thank you, Miss Mary," Annie said.

Miss Mary. Mary Fields had been called a lot of things, but rarely that. She cackled louder than the hens as she lifted the reins and urged the team into action.

• • •

The next day, Mary rode into Cascade for the sisters' mail and other essentials. One such essential took her to the Silver Dollar.

"You out raising hell, Mary?" The barkeeper took the empty clay jug from the only woman he allowed to drink in his saloon.

"Hell still far below us, and a long ways off," she replied. "Though there's some that do their best to create it here on earth."

"That's the truth," he said.

"Driving outta the mill, I took a shortcut down an old wagon trail. Terrible road. Spied a sweet homestead above the creek. Like to have me a pretty spot like that someday."

"Must be Charles Burnham's place. That son of a gun wants it both ways. Farming's too much work, so he's got that Indian woman he calls a wife to prove up his claim while he cowboys it up, staying out weeks at a time." The barkeeper set a glass of liquid the color of willow bark in front of her, then refilled her jug.

Mary let out a low rumble. "That satisfy the law?"

He snorted. "Maybe not back East. But the lawmen and agents around here ain't too particular. Especially when it comes to white men and Indian women."

That told Mary what she needed to know.

• • •

"Doesn't take long without a working laundry to make us thank the Lord for such comforts, does it, Mary?" The white wimple attached to her black veil and the stiff white collar covering her chest gave Mother Amadeus Dunne a stern look that hid a kind heart.

"No, it surely don't." Mary couldn't bring herself to call a white woman "Mother," especially one more than a dozen years younger. She'd been Theresa to the Dunne family but "Miss Theresa" to the servants, and Mary still thought of her that way. At fifty-three or thereabouts, Mary was older than everyone else at the Mission. She wasn't keen on calling the young Jesuits "Father," either, so she avoided calling them anything. In truth, she avoided them as much as she could, fearing they would take any opportunity to report her slightest misdeeds to Bishop Brondel in Helena. Mother Amadeus had already run interference more than once, knowing Mary hadn't caused half the trouble people laid at her feet.

"Now we can finish the dormitory," Mother Amadeus said. "We can't keep cramming our pupils into the old log cabins or their parents will take them home, and that will be the end of their education."

For the few white girls who boarded. Mary expected the

Indian parents would be more tolerant of the rough conditions, most of them sleeping on pallets in hide-covered tipis or wooden shacks. They already had twelve Indian girls boarding and twenty settlers' girls, most of those day students. Building supplies and good labor were hard to come by. But Amadeus had promised the bishop a school for girls, and she kept her promises.

Mary hitched Peter and Paul to the wagon and headed out to fetch another load of boards and timbers, the black-and-white dog beside her. Montana Territory didn't look much like the Tennessee hills where she'd been reared. So dry, except along the creeks and the Missouri, not yet the great river it became downstream. The whispering leaves of a cottonwood or a willow nearly made her weep, and she didn't expect to ever see an oak or beech forest again. But the land bore a soft sheen that hadn't been there just a few weeks ago, and the prairie sage carried a sharp scent, not unpleasant. Patches of tiny white and yellow flowers bloomed where the road carved through a slope.

Mary turned onto the little-used trail. Shorter as the crow flies, but narrow and rutted, it made a hard drive and one she would not take under threatening skies. But she had a yearning to see young Josie, and to check on the girl's mother.

"Whoa, there, Peter," she bellowed as she neared the homestead. The horses slowed and she cocked her head, listening. Land can carry a feeling, if you pay attention.

"Get along with you. Don't be stopping here." A man stepped out of the high grasses on the uphill side of the trail where the wild shrubs were sparse, his britches tucked into tall boots, his face reddened by the sun.

"Horses need water," Mary said, though she'd let the pair drink not far back. No decent man would deny a horse water, no matter how much he despised their driver.

The man stared, deciding. "Pull up yonder, then. I got an old trough, so you don't have to unhitch 'em."

If she'd been a white man, he'd have been happy to help her unhitch the pair, and offered her a bucket and ladle as Annie had done. But hard as life could be at times, Mary had never once wished to be a white man.

"Miss Mary, you came back!" Josie's voice rang out. The girl, again in the blue calico, stood at the break in the brush, bouncing on her bare feet. Then she saw her father on the other side of the road. The bouncing stopped, and the narrow shoulders sank.

Mary turned back to Burnham. His blue eyes had narrowed into thin slits. He'd set the butt of his Winchester on the ground, but his fingers tightened around the barrel.

"Mr. Burnham, I bought eggs off your wife last week, and I was hoping to buy a few more. For the sisters."

"We can't spare none," Burnham said. "If you can't raise enough for 'em, you don't deserve your keep."

Mary kept her gaze level. On the seat next to her, the dog growled softly.

"Pa," Josie said, her voice high and strained, "the sisters are running a school for girls. I could go and learn how to read, since you don't have time to teach me, and how to—"

"You're not going. I told you once already, and that's the end of it. Your ma needs you, especially with the baby on the way."

Mary squinted. Was that a cut on the girl's face, and a fresh bruise?

"How is Miss Annie?" she asked.

A shadow crossed Burnham's face. "Poorly," he admitted. "But she'll perk up once the baby comes, in a few weeks."

"Let her come to the convent. Some of the sisters have training as nurses." Not strictly true, but stretching the truth now and then didn't hurt, when it aimed to help someone. "She and Josie will be well taken care of. You can visit, then head out to the range without worrying."

"Say yes, Pa. Maybe I can start at the school. Maybe—"

"I said no. That ain't the place for you." His words slapped the girl as sharply as if he'd reached across the road, past the big Black woman in the wagon, past the full-chested horses in their harnesses, and struck her. She froze, eyes filled with terror and tears she dared not cry.

He turned to Mary. A vein throbbed in his neck and his nostrils flared. "Can't think why they put up with you, the way you quarrel with the priests and drink like a man."

The heat rose up inside of her. She gathered all her might to shove it back down. She had no trouble letting loose with her temper when it suited her, but she could not do so now. Not if she wanted Annie and Josie in a safe place when the baby came. What sort of man wouldn't want a safe childbed for his wife?

A man who feared losing what little power he had in the world—power over a defenseless young woman and a daughter who longed to learn and be loved.

A man who did not deserve them.

Likely he would punish the girl when Mary left, but nothing good would come of lingering.

"Thank you for offering water for the horses, Mr. Burnham," she said, though he had not offered until she asked, and begrudgingly at that. "If I remember right, this trail cuts down to the creek a ways up. I'll let them drink their fill there. Good day to you."

Mary glanced back at Josie, a pang in her heart. She patted the dog and clucked at the horses, and the wagon moved on.

• • •

A few days later, Mary made the trip again. This time, besides the dog, she'd brought one of the younger nuns. "Girl could use a little fresh air—she a bit peaked," Mary had told Mother Amadeus when asking if Sister Louisine could accompany her.

Amadeus had given Mary a skeptical look, glancing first at Louisine, the picture of health, then back to Mary before nodding approval. The young nun had grabbed her skirts and clambered into the wagon without waiting for a hand up.

"I am learning to love this land, strange as it first seemed," Louisine said now as Mary steered the workhorses out of the Mission. "The buttes and gullies, the horizon so far away. The hills dotted with pines. And the mountains—oh, my. Their peaks pierce your heart, don't they, so sharp and rugged. As though they want nothing more than to reach the heavens in the hopes of touching the Lord. We should all be reaching like that."

Louisine chatted like a girl headed to a dance, but in truth, she made pleasant company, and if her expressions of delight in discovering her surroundings were fanciful, they brought the older woman satisfaction nonetheless.

At the mill, Mary finished her sandwiches while Louisine visited with the owner's wife inside a white clapboard house. Two small boys ran around the log yard, careful to keep their distance from the broad-shouldered Black woman.

She leaned against the side of the wagon and drew on her cigar. The smell of tobacco comforted her, and mingled with the scent of spruce and pine that clung to the air. She kept a close eye on Whitney, the millwright, and his hired man, making sure they gave the nuns the quality the bishop was paying for. Weren't nobody gonna pass a gnarled timber under her eyes.

"You will send them to the school in a few years, won't

you?" Louisine said as she strolled toward the wagon with Mrs. Whitney. The younger boy stopped to pet Mary's dog, while the older, Thomas, watched the two men slide in the last timbers.

"I thought the mission schools were for Indian children," Mrs. Whitney said.

"The Jesuits educate ranch boys as well as Indians," Louisine said. "Separately, of course. And the Ursuline sisters have charge of the girls. Your boys will be in good hands."

"We'll see then, in time," the woman said, and thanked the young nun for the visit.

"I do believe it does a woman good to see another woman once in a while." Louisine waved goodbye as Mary pulled the wagon away. "Growing up with three older sisters, and my grandmother and spinster aunt in the house, I would scarce know how to live apart from other women."

Long as they didn't all chatter like Louisine, Mary thought. One tweety bird was fine; spare her the flock.

A mile from the mill, Mary turned the heavy wagon off the main road. Louisine glanced at her but said nothing, wide eyes taking in the untamed country.

They reached the low spot where the trail dipped near the creek, its rushing waters hidden by wild roses. "Take a breather, Paul. Slow you down, Peter," Mary shouted. One horse whinnied. Mercifully, Louisine held her tongue.

And there was the girl, at the gap in the thicket, summoned by the wagon's rattle and Mary's calls. As the horses stopped, Annie trod heavily up the path.

"Hello, Miss Mary," Josie said, then clapped her hand over her mouth at the sight of Louisine in her strange outfit.

"Josie," Mary said. "Miss Annie. This is Sister Louisine. She's a city girl, and I'm giving her an eyeful."

"She surely is," Louisine said. "What a lovely spot. I can't get over how varied this country is. Do you know, in Ohio, the forests grow so thick you can hardly push through them? Of course, the trees aren't like these—they're hardwood, and in the autumn, when the leaves turn—oh, my." She clasped her hands to her chest. They were fine and pretty, thanks to the balm she rubbed in them every night. Mary had helped her procure a supply, with an unspoken promise not to tell the other sisters, who would either clamor for their own or chide the novice for her vanity.

Vain she might be, but Mary had noticed the young woman's sharp gaze settle on Josie's bruised forearm and take in Annie's worn look, her face thinner than when they'd met.

"Mary." Louisine turned and touched the older woman's black shirtsleeve, made for a man but just right for her. "Do say we have time to visit." Not waiting for an answer, she gathered her skirts and jumped down.

Mary kept her smile to herself.

"Is your husband home?" Louisine took Annie's arm and they started down the path to the cabin.

"No, ma'am, Sister. He runs cattle."

"I had never heard of open range before coming West. They run loose for months?"

"Yes, ma'am. But he keeps a careful eye on them, riding out and sleeping with the herd."

Kinder to his cattle than to his womenfolk, Mary thought as she climbed out of the wagon. Oh, for a young woman's knees. She had little doubt that Burnham's chief worry was thieves, not his cattle's well-being, though even a man as hard as he would know healthy stock fetched a better price than ailing animals.

Josie watched Mary unhitch the team.

"She's a nun, ain't she? Is she a teacher?"

"You don't have to whisper, child," Mary said. "Yes, she

is. Now get your bucket and we'll get us some cold creek water."

The woman and girl filled the trough, then each took a ladle themselves and let the horses drink. Josie showed Mary the garden patch and chicken coop, a rickety structure that looked like a fox could knock it over with his tail. The girl was counting eggs into Mary's basket when Annie and Louisine emerged from the cabin, the nun pausing to finger the pale pink hollyhocks by the door. Her habit swished in the grass, and the chickens clucked as they circled round her.

Mary shot the young nun a look, then counted coins into Josie's hand.

The girl closed her fingers and gazed up with a brightness that had been lacking on Mary's last visit. On the day Charles Burnham had trampled his daughter's hopes.

Mary tucked the eggs into the basket she'd brought along and hitched up the team.

Louisine took Annie's hands. "You're sure you and Josie won't come with us."

"Please, Mama," Josie said, but Annie kept her head down and shook it slowly.

"Then we'll keep you in our prayers, for a safe delivery and confinement."

Confinement, Mary thought. That's a luxury no country woman had, nor most city women, neither.

"I can't promise to come along the next time Mary picks up a load, but I'll try." From her seat beside Mary, Louisine lifted the small cross at the end of the long rosary hanging from her waist. She signed, first in Annie's direction, the woman signing with her, then Josie's. The girl's small brown hand could not follow the movements, weaving like a cowboy after a night in the Silver Dollar.

Mary whistled and the dog jumped in. She called to the horses and off they rolled.

It was half a mile or more before the silence broke.

"You sly woman, you," Louisine said. "A bird could fly through the gaps between the planks of that cabin. Plenty of fresh water, but it has to be hauled up by hand. She has no women around, and no medical supplies, though she does better at keeping things clean and tidy with next to nothing than most women with a laundry house and hired help. The tradesman did come by, but her husband sent him away."

"You see what he's done to the girl."

"Half-broken her spirit, as well as her cheekbone. The mother, too." The nun sighed. "I'm no midwife, but I did tend to my sister with both her babies. Annie's pulses are too fast and too full. Her feet and ankles are badly swollen. There's a deep bruise yellowing on her neck, and a fresh one on her wrist. He must have ridden out only a day or two ago."

"You, Peter, Paul. Move a little faster, now," Mary called roughly. The horses were used to heavy loads, and to their driver, and they kept the same steady pace even as she tightened the reins.

"Tell me, Mary, did you bring me along as nurse, or witness?"

Mary kept her eyes on the trail, and Louisine sighed again.

"The law says a woman belongs to her husband. He can do as he likes. Of course, we don't know that they are married, but that makes no difference. The law cares even less about Indian women than white women, and that's not saying much." She grew quiet, but not for long. "You know my father is a judge, acquainted with Mother Amadeus's brother, Judge Dunne, and that's how I came to join her order. I admired her deeply, and happily accepted the call to head West."

Mary knew. She had counted on the young woman's knowledge of the law, as well as her gentle nature and her natural sympathies toward other women. Not every nun could see past the faces of a different color to the heart that beat beneath the skin, to the soul that longed for the same God they all longed for.

Louisine laid her hand on Mary's. She bent her head and murmured a prayer, barely audible, though Mary made out the words "courage" and "protection."

Then the young nun sat back, hands folded in her lap, and on the long drive home, the two women worked out a plan.

• • •

A surprise visit from the bishop triggered a flurry of cooking, cleaning, and other chores at St. Peter's, and kept Mary from driving out the old trail for nearly two weeks. Mother Amadeus was none too pleased with another request for Louisine's company, until the young nun took her superior aside and spoke in tones Mary could not hear.

Well before they reached the homestead, the two women fell into a heavy-hearted silence. As Mary drove the team around the last curve, Louisine raised her black-robed arm and pointed.

On the hilltop stood a cross, three feet high. Mary peered over the sage to see a second, smaller cross. Though the wood was weathered, the mound of dirt was newly dug.

A shiver rippled through her, despite the warm day.

She cleared her throat and shouted at the horses. By the time the team had slowed, Charles Burnham stood by the trail, rifle in hand, Josie peering from behind him.

"Please accept our condolences, Mr. Burnham," Louisine said.

Josie stifled a sob, and Burnham's Adam's apple bobbed.

"I'd have brought her to town, or to the sisters, but by the time I got here . . ." Burnham's voice broke, then trailed off.

"Annie was alone? With no one but the girl?" Louisine's voice rose, her face as pale as her collar.

"There weren't nothing no one could do," Burnham said, growing louder and defiant. "Not for seizures. Not when a body just won't wake."

Symptoms of a not-uncommon complication, Mary knew, one often fatal. But there was no excuse for leaving the woman alone with a child, forced to watch her mother die. Rage welled up in Mary's throat. She studied Josie's face, the girl's eyes red-rimmed, her skin splotchy.

"You and your daughter will be in all the sisters' prayers," Louisine said. "Let us share in your burden."

Burnham's eyes blazed. "If you mean take my daughter to that mission and fill her mind with foolishness, you turn around and drive right on back."

"We would be pleased to help you with Josie's education, Mr. Burnham," Louisine said in a soothing tone. "But you would always remain her father."

"Damn you, women. Get on out of here." He lifted the rifle and held it with both hands.

On the wagon seat, Mary shifted slightly. Burnham glanced her way. The barrel of the pistol in her lap glinted in the sun.

He raised his chin, eyes wary. "Go ahead. Shoot me. You'll hang by nightfall."

"I ain't worried about hanging," Mary said. "The good Lord will take care of me. My soul will pass yours, heading the other direction."

His eyes flashed and he breathed out heavily before lowering the rifle. Sister Louisine raised one hand. Then she meted out the justice the two women had devised, anticipating both calamity and resistance. "Mr. Burnham, we will take Josie to the school. You will pay five dollars a month for her keep." St. Peter's did not charge tuition or fees, and only those who could were expected to pay for room and board, but Mary and Louisine had concluded that requiring a regular donation would be fair, and Mother Amadeus had agreed. Penance.

"She will stay with the sisters until she finishes high school and teachers' training. You will visit every first Sunday and on Easter. You will say not one harsh word to her about your late wife."

"And I get what?"

"You save your soul, Mr. Burnham, for God is a harsher judge than the law in some cases."

His jaw tightened. "Get your things," he told the girl, and she turned and ran toward the cabin.

Mary kept one eye on Burnham's rifle while Sister Louisine recited the details of the school's curriculum and the opportunities the Ursulines would provide. Josie rushed up the path, a small bundle in one hand, a reed basket in the other. Mary settled the girl in the wagon between the two women, the dog in back.

She kept her hand on her pistol until they were far out of Burnham's sight.

"You've done a good deed, Mary," Louisine said. "You shall be blest in heaven."

Mary grunted. "The Bible says God watches over the sparrows. But I figure even He can use a little help from time to time."

MISS STARR'S GOODBYE

"Sarah, you are coming home with me, and that is final." The slender man in the black suit stomped his heeled boot on the boardwalk, and the vibration rattled the planks all the way to where Josie stood, in front of the Cascade Mercantile. Three horse lengths. Josie didn't know how to figure that in regular numbers.

"And I told you, James McCumber, I am going nowhere." The woman called Sarah raised her chin defiantly, the reddest rose Josie had ever seen nestled in her pile of chestnut hair. Was the rose real? Sarah perched her hands on her hips, her waist impossibly narrow, her blouse impossibly white. "This is my home now."

"This godforsaken backwater? Sarah, you were meant for better things. For a refined, respectable life."

Josie felt Mary stiffen beside her. Folks from all over came to Cascade on Saturday afternoons, as they had, to pick up the mail and supplies, and catch up on the talk. It was a hot, sticky day, midway through August, a brief lull before the last push to bring in the hay and other crops. The shouting had lured everyone out of the shops and businesses, even the sheriff, standing in the doorway of the sandstone jail across the dirt street.

Miss Starr's Goodbye

"By respectable, you mean marrying a man I don't love, being at his beck and call, one more shiny object for him to brag about? No, James. If you want to take me back to Philadelphia, you might as well kill me first. Because a life in a gilded cage would be the death of me." Sarah shook her head, the magnificent hair somehow staying put. She caught sight of Mary and threw her a big smile. "And Montana's not godforsaken, is it, Mary? How many nuns live at St. Peter's Mission now? Half a dozen or more? And a pair of priests, with an honest-to-goodness bishop just up the river in Helena. They pray for us all. Even me."

"Miss Starr," Mary replied. "Good to see you."

"It's not enough," James said, his face flushed, "that you're living in a den of iniquity. You're friends with Negroes, too?"

"I am friends with whom I please," the woman replied. She cocked one hip, the folds of her dark red velvet skirt swaying. "And when I please a certain kind of friend, I am paid quite well." With her last words, her voice and eyes grew sharp.

Mary reached for Josie's hand. "Mother Amadeus would kill me for letting you hear such talk." She tugged Josie past the store, where other onlookers were beginning to shuffle their feet and look uncomfortable.

"Mary, what's a qunninity?"

"A what?" Mary said as they turned the corner from Main on to First Street. "Oh, hush, child. If I'd known you were going to ask so many questions . . ."

But what she would have done had she known, the big Black woman didn't say. They had reached their destination.

• • •

"Now Mary, you know I ain't got no problem with you coming in to quench your thirst, but that girl . . ." The mustachioed man behind the bar in the Silver Dollar shook his head. "Can't be lettin' her in."

Mary shook the dust from her black skirt, the pistol she always carried heavy in her pocket. The black-and-white dog at her heels sneezed.

Two men hunched over the bar craned their necks to stare, no doubt spoiling to see if she'd pick a fight. She ought to. She was a sturdy woman with a broad face and dark skin, catching narrowed looks for her size and her color. Every man within a day's drive of Cascade, Montana, knew she carried a pistol in her pocket, and she didn't mind that most folks thought she'd use it without much provocation.

If Josie were a white boy, nobody would blink an eye at seeing her in the saloon on a Saturday afternoon. If she were a white girl, the barkeeper would tell Mary to send her down to the general store for penny candy, and maybe sneak her a coin or two.

But a half-breed was another story, even one in a plain cotton dress and white pinafore, and shoes on her feet.

Mary's throat cramped, dusty and dry. Weren't no use fighting things that weren't going to change. She turned to the girl, still straddling the threshold. "You go down to the river, Josie. See if you can scare up some wildflowers for the sisters. Keep outta trouble, you hear?"

"Yes, Miss Mary." Josie's voice rang out clear, and Mary heard a snicker from a table in the corner shadows. The girl's footfalls echoed as she ran across the wide plank porch and down the wooden steps, fading to nothing as she reached the dusty street. Mary marched to the bar and wrapped her thick, calloused fingers around the whiskey glass.

• • •

Josie's shoes pinched, but she was not going to take them off. Shoes meant she was somebody. A pupil at the Ursuline school at St. Peter, twelve miles northwest of town. A boarder, her mother dead and her father busy with his cattle. She knew some white folks scoffed at the idea of educating Indian children. But Mother Amadeus, the woman Mary always called "Miss Theresa," would have none of that. She'd come West to teach Indian girls at the request of the Jesuit priests, and Mary said that when Miss Theresa got the bit in her teeth, weren't no stopping her.

At the corner, Josie paused. The river lay to her right. But she had only been to town a few times and hadn't seen it all, so she made a left, hopping up onto the boardwalk as a wide wagon, laden with supplies, rumbled past.

Mary had taken her into the general store earlier in the day, the nuns' list of supplies in hand. She'd felt the other customers' eyes on them, the big Black woman and the small girl, one-quarter Blackfeet. But not all the folks had been unfriendly. It was Mary who drove the wagon into town every Saturday, and sometimes delivered mail or supplies for folks living near the Mission who couldn't get away. It was Mary who went for the doctor or the priest, and folks who knew her trusted her.

When Josie paused in front of the glass candy jars, Mary had frowned and pulled her away. Now, Josie thought she might go in for another look. She didn't have any money, but a look was almost as sweet as the taste itself.

"Hey, you half-breed. Get on home," a rough male voice shouted, and Josie froze. With all the people coming and going, she couldn't see who had yelled at her. Her cheeks grew hot with shame, and she darted around the corner, another shout and sharp laughter following her.

Partway down the alley, she stopped, breathless, flattening

herself in a doorway. Mary had told her to stay out of trouble, to go down to the river. Why hadn't she listened?

She stood in the shadows for a long time, until her heart quieted and her breath calmed. The nuns said when you quieted the voices inside you, you could hear the whisper of God. You could hear it in the church, of course, but also in the willows and the songs of the sparrows and the meadowlark.

But that wasn't what Josie heard now. A loud voice, its volume matched by another. Both male. She leaned forward ever so slowly, but the alley was empty. The shouting continued and she glanced up. A window stood open on the third floor of the hotel across the alley, its board siding painted a soft buttery yellow.

Cascade is the fightingest town, she thought. The harsh tones made her insides jump, like she'd swallowed a live grasshopper. Like when her father had shouted at her mother and hit them both. It never took much to set him off—too many flies in the outhouse, the ladle slipping into the bucket, the rooster crowing when he shouldn't have. She loved her pa, and she often cried herself to sleep over missing her ma, but living with the nuns was good. She still had chores to do, and the sewing needle pricked the tips of her fingers bloody red, but she was learning to read and write and do simple sums. And Mary and the younger nun called Louisine always made sure she got enough to eat.

The voices broke into her thoughts, and she gazed up at the window again. The dark-haired man in the black suit—wasn't he the man who'd been arguing with the pretty lady in the street? James, she had called him. James McCumber. A hand came into view, one finger pointed at James, who backed out of sight as the finger-pointing man appeared in the window. He was taller than James, and stockier, his thick hair the color of golden wheat. But far away as she was, Josie only picked up snatches of what they said. Nothing that made sense.

Then the window was empty. Josie had no idea how long she'd been standing here, but surely long enough for the man who'd taunted her on the street to be gone. She crept down the alley silently, her hands scraping on the mercantile's white clapboard as she peered around the corner.

"Why, hello, little girl!" a voice boomed, and Josie jumped six inches. The voice came from behind her, and it belonged to the golden-haired man she'd seen in the window.

"He–hello," she said. "Sir."

He crouched, lowering himself to her height. "Who are we spying on?" he whispered, his gaze flicking playfully to the boardwalk.

"No–nobody." Josie's braids flew as she shook her head.

Golden Hair laughed and straightened. "It's all right, little bird. Your secret's safe with me." He reached a hand into the pocket of his dark brown trousers and tossed her a silver coin. "Don't spend it all in one place." Then he winked, and sauntered off down the boardwalk.

Josie stared, open-mouthed, at the coin in her hand. Could she, dare she? She glanced up and down the street. No sign of Mary. She dashed around the corner and into the store.

A few minutes later, the treasure in her pocket, Josie wandered down to the river, praying Mary would not be waiting. Mary liked to take her time in the saloon, but sometimes she came out cross. Her dark moods never lasted long, not around Josie, anyway, but better not to have to tiptoe around them.

The flat sandstone ledge where Mary liked to sit was warmed by the summer sun and cooled by the river breeze. Josie clambered up, the soles of her shoes slipping a bit, then sat and pulled the peppermint stick out of her pocket.

The sun and the sweet must have made her drowsy, because she didn't hear Mary approach until the big woman's foot struck a loose rock and sent it tumbling down the riverbank. Josie stuffed the candy in her skirt pocket and wiped her mouth with the back of her hand.

"Oh, these old bones," Mary said, settling herself next to Josie. She set the clay jug, stoppered with a birch plug, between them, but didn't take a drink. Instead, she pulled a soft buckskin pouch out of her skirts and withdrew a pipe and tin. She held the pipe away from her, squinting, lips pursed, as she tamped tobacco into the bowl. She struck a match on the rock, lit up, and took a deep draw. Leaned against the sandstone bluff behind them. "Oh, that is fine."

They sat in silence as Mary smoked and Josie watched the white pelicans drift along on the currents below them. Funny birds, their orange beaks longer than their necks, their wing and tail feathers dipped in ink. Mary had been all up and down this river, the mighty Missouri, and said it was wider and not so still downstream. Josie thought it was paradise.

"Mary," she said. "You knew that lady in the street, didn't you?"

"What lady? Oh-h-h, Miss Starr." Mary chuckled. "There are some don't call her a lady."

"Why didn't she want to go home? Doesn't everyone want to go home?"

Mary lowered her pipe and turned to study her. "Do you want to go home, child? Back to your daddy's cabin on Trout Creek?"

"No!" Josie felt herself flush. "No, I mean the Mission. That's my home. Where my cot is, and the chickens I take care of, and the school books and my slate. But Miss Starr told the man she didn't want to go home. Was he her husband?"

"Miss Starr ain't got no husband. Reckon that's what the set-to was about. Could be that man—"

"James. She called him James McCumber."

"I believe James McCumber is Miss Starr's brother, sent out by the family to return her to the fold."

"Is her name really Starr?" Josie said. "Like in the sky? And is it her first name or her last? He called her Sarah."

Mary drew on the pipe again. "You and your questions. She goes by the one name, Starr. It ain't the name her mama and pappy gave her, but the name she chose. That's real enough for me."

"You mean she changed it?" Josie tucked one leg beneath her. "Like the nuns changed their names, to signify entering a new life and giving themselves to God?"

Mary started coughing, and leaned forward to clear her throat. After several minutes, she straightened, wiping her cheek with her fingertips.

"I think Miss Starr is like Mother Amadeus," Josie said. "Amadeus is the name she wants St. Peter to call when it's her time to go to heaven, so that's the name she uses at the Mission. But you knew her in Ohio, so she lets you call her Miss Theresa. That's her home name, like Miss Starr's brother calls her Sarah."

"Oh, Lordy, child. Ain't nothing wrong with your mind." Mary emptied the bowl of her pipe into the brush beside the rock, then tucked it away. "That sun be high in the sky. Time to hitch up the horses and wagon, and load our supplies."

Josie patted her pocket for the peppermint stick and jumped off the rock. She'd witnessed two fights, gotten a silver coin, and bought herself a piece of candy, all in one day.

You never knew what would happen on a day with Mary.

• • •

Mary would have relished Josie's company the next Saturday—her questions were more amusing than annoying—but the pupils were picking chokecherries today for winter jelly. So Mary drove the team toward town alone, her and the dog. She liked being alone. Before the war, when she was property, she'd rarely been alone and never got the chance to make her own choices, even after she was growed. The war gave her rights, but it hadn't given her a lot of choices.

Wanting to make their own choices might be the only thing she had in common with Miss Starr, but it was a powerful bond. Still, she knew the ache that came from disappointing those who loved you.

She dropped off a basket of fresh bread and butter for a farmer whose wife had died the previous spring. The poor man was struggling a bit with the young'uns, but the neighbors and nuns kept an eye out. And his fields looked good—he wouldn't suffer a crop loss to boot.

She pulled the wagon into the corral at the edge of town, and she and the stable master took a look at the gray's hind leg. They pried out a stone lodged between shoe and hoof. "You keep an eye on that shoe," he warned her, and she grunted. No point telling him she'd been driving a team since before he was born.

At the Mercantile, she dropped off the nuns' supply list and picked up a new tin of tobacco, as well as the face cream one of the young nuns was partial to. Mary didn't mind keeping the girl's secret—face cream weren't no big sin, even if Miss Theresa wouldn't approve. Miss Theresa had already left her family home and professed her vows when Mary came to work for her brother, but that didn't mean Mary didn't know a few of her secrets, too.

In the Silver Dollar, the barkeeper set her glass of rye at the end of the bar. A few sips in, the door opened and a stocky man in a brown suit with hair the color of ripe wheat entered, three men in city black with waistcoats and watch chains in tow. They settled at a scarred, round table near her, and the man in the brown suit called to the bartender for a bottle of his best whiskey.

"My friends and I are celebrating a new business venture," he said.

Mary watched in the mirror as the bartender set the bottle and four glasses on the table. "What kinda venture, if I may ask?"

"A good, solid cash business," he replied, and one of his friends chuckled. "Providing necessary services." More laughter.

"Ain't seen you fellows before," the bartender said. "Where you planning on setting up this business?"

"Down in Helena," one of the men said, though he pronounced the name of the capital Hell-EE-na, marking him new to the territory. "Plenty of money and plenty of demand. By the time statehood comes around, our reputation will be unsullied."

The three men in black cackled again, reaching for their glasses.

"Just a few bumps in the road," the leader of the crew said. "Nothing a little persuasion can't work out."

A dark look crossed his sunburned face, disappearing so quickly Mary wasn't sure she'd seen it. He had a kind of ruthlessness she remembered too well, the kind of cruel determination to get your way that she'd seen on the faces of men with whips in hand.

He raised his glass. "Gentlemen, a toast to the Eastern Star."

A mine, a rail line? Could be either one. Mary kept one eye on the men as she sipped her whiskey. Something about them—about the man in the brown suit—made her wary. He was clearly the talker in the foursome, and his companions laughed at his stories, but she noticed how their eyes narrowed as they flicked towards him, not matching their too-broad smiles. Whoever he was, whatever yarns he was spinning, they didn't quite trust him, either.

She drained her drink, set the empty glass on the bar, and looped one finger through the handle of her jug. Time to check on the horses and leave these natterin' men behind.

• • •

The next week, Josie helped Mary unhitch the horses at the town stables so they could get a good drink and rest a bit. The corral was about half as full as on their last visit. As Josie began to brush the chestnut, the stable master approached to inspect the gray's hoof.

"Looks good," he pronounced as he straightened. "I'll say this for you, Mary. You got a good hand with a team."

Mary led him away and they spoke, out of earshot. When she returned, the grim set to her mouth troubled Josie, and she promised God in her heart that if she'd upset Mary, she would not spend the coins safely tucked in her pocket on another peppermint stick, but would give them to Mother Amadeus instead.

On their way to the Mercantile, Josie was surprised to see the streets so quiet. Inside, the shop was empty except for a woman sorting through bolts of calico while her husband waited, a worried expression on his face. Mary handed the shopkeeper their list without a word. Mr. Whitney, he was called. His brother ran the lumber mill and came to the Mission sometimes.

Mr. Whitney the grocer looked over the list, said he had everything she needed in stock, and he'd box it up for her.

Then he smiled at Josie and pointed at the candy jars. Josie opened her mouth, but Mary grabbed her hand and hustled her away before she could answer his unspoken question.

Outside, Mary finally found her tongue. "Child, I've got an unpleasant errand to run. Things are ugly in town right now, and I don't want you wandering around by yourself. You got to come with me, and be real quiet and real good."

Josie got shivery inside, like when the dark clouds built up in the western sky and you knew a storm was coming, but you didn't know when or how wild it would be. "What is it, Mary? What's happened? Is that why the people stayed home?"

"Ain't no use trying to keep anything from you, is there?" Mary huffed out a long slow breath. "I reckon you'll figure it out soon enough. The man you saw arguing in the street with his sister?"

"Mr. James and Miss Starr," Josie said.

Mary clucked, a disapproving sound. "James McCumber was found stabbed to death last Thursday night, downriver a ways. Fool sheriff's gone and arrested his sister."

"Miss Starr? Did she do it, Mary? Did she kill her brother?" The thought was both thrilling and horrifying.

But Mary didn't answer. She waited for a wagon to roll by, then stepped off the boardwalk and headed for the jail, Josie running behind.

Outside the jail, Mary pointed to a bench and Josie sat, swinging her feet while Mary trudged up the wooden steps and pushed open the door. She sat for the longest time, but Mary did not return. Her bottom grew all wiggly until she couldn't sit one more minute. She stood on the bench and peeked in through the glass window. Inside, the sheriff's office was dark and gloomy. The sheriff sat with his feet on the desk, his tan, dirt-scuffed hat pulled over his face.

Josie shielded her eyes with her hands and made out a metal door, shut tight, a lock through the hasp. Had they locked Mary up, too? Or was she behind the door, talking with Miss Starr?

Josie jumped down and walked around the side of the building. In the rear, well above her head, iron bars covered a window. No glass. It must get cold in there, she thought. Would they keep Miss Starr through the winter? Or would they hang her? Josie had heard talk of hangings, back when she lived in the cabin with her parents and a tradesman had stopped to pass the time of day with her pa. Hanging sounded terrible, worse than anything she could imagine. But it's what they did to killers.

A hot, sharp burst of fear ran through her.

She leaned against the warm stone wall. Words drifted out from inside, and she recognized the voice as Miss Starr's.

"You've got to believe me. I could not let James haul me back to Philadelphia and enslave me in a so-called life of respectability, but I did not kill my brother. Oh, Mary, forgive me. I shouldn't have said it like that."

Josie could not hear Mary's reply, but Miss Starr's next words came through clearly. "He arrested me to show me he's in charge."

"Why he want to do that?" Mary said. "He know you valuable to this town. Men got to come in to drink and resupply, but they stay overnight in the hotel because they want to visit you. And he makes his share, don't he?"

"Oh, he does, and that's where the trouble started. He jacked up his take. It was pure extortion." Miss Starr sounded agitated, her voice moving in and out of Josie's hearing. Pacing, she thought. "I'm a businesswoman. I made other plans."

Why would Miss Starr need to pay the sheriff? Josie slapped a fly away from her face.

"That may be," Mary answered, "but unless you come up with a better explanation for why your brother be dead, one nobody can deny, you gonna swing."

"Oh, Mary. You know how it is to be blamed for things you didn't do." Miss Starr had apparently heard Josie's silent urging to stand still, close to the window, giving Josie a better chance to hear her. "You've got to help me."

"Don't know how, but I'll try."

Josie dashed back to the front of the building and sat on the bench. A few minutes later, Mary emerged, the sleepy sheriff in the doorway behind her.

"You heard her threaten him," he said. "Two weeks ago, right there in the middle of the street. Half the county heard her."

"I heard no such thing," Mary replied, her voice low and sure. "I heard a woman say she meant to be in charge of her own life. That don't mean she'd kill her brother."

"Judge is due a week from Monday," the sheriff said. "Then we'll have justice."

Mary held out a hand for Josie, and they marched down the street toward the river. "Justice, my eye," she muttered. "That no-count lawman wouldn't know justice if it bit him in the bee-hind."

They climbed up to the rock ledge and sat. Mary pulled out her buckskin pouch and held the pipe in her hand, but didn't fill it. Josie didn't know whether to tell Mary what she'd heard and risk being punished for eavesdropping, or hold her tongue, as both Mary and Mother Amadeus often told her to do.

"Child, Miss Starr in a heap o' trouble," Mary finally said, her voice heavy. "She say she didn't kill her brother, and I want to believe her, but how can I? We heard her arguing with him, and we heard her say she'd die before going back to

Philadelphia with him. So did they argue again? Did they struggle and she stab him, like the sheriff say?" Mary made a stabbing motion with her fist, still clutching the bowl of her pipe.

"You always say I ask too many questions, Mary, but it sounds like you've got plenty of your own."

Mary stuck the pipe in her mouth to keep herself from laughing.

"Mary," Josie continued. "If I tell you something, and by the telling you know I disobeyed you, will it still be a sin and will you still punish me?"

"Child, what are you going on about?"

"I—I might have heard something that could help Miss Starr."

"Well, don't just sit there. Tell me."

Josie told Mary about hearing Mr. James and the man with the golden hair arguing in the hotel.

Mary frowned. "You make out anything they said?"

"Just that—just that Mr. James was talking about the train to Philadelphia, and the other man laughed in his face. He said"—Josie broke off, trying to remember—"he said something about going to hell."

"Well, that don't narrow it down much. You think you recognize this man, if you see him again?"

"Oh, yes." Josie's head bobbed up and down. "He gave me a silver coin." She clapped her hand over her mouth. She shouldn't have said that. Now she was really going to be in trouble.

But Mary was tucking her pipe back in the buckskin bag— she hadn't even filled it, let alone smoked it—then she put a hand on Josie's shoulder and pushed herself up. "Come on, child. You've got to tell that story again, and pray it be enough."

Josie scrambled to her feet and followed Mary back to town. Never had she seen the big woman move so fast.

A few minutes later, when she'd finished telling him what she'd seen, the sheriff squinted at her, then turned his attention to Mary. His hands lay flat on the small wooden desk, next to a knife with a carved bone handle and a steel blade.

"Now, why should I believe some tale you cooked up with this half-breed to try to save a murdering whore from the rope?"

Josie felt the blood rush from her head, then Mary's hand on her shoulder, steadying her.

"Because it's the truth. She took that silver coin the man tossed her and bought herself a peppermint stick in the Mercantile. I smelled it on her breath. You ask Mr. Whitney. He'll remember."

The sheriff glared up at Mary, then turned his hard stare back to Josie. "You spend it all on candy?"

"No, sir." Josie dug in her pocket and drew out a lump of grimy white cotton. She untied the square, a wobbly letter J embroidered in white on one corner, to reveal two small coins, the change from her purchase. The first purchase she'd ever made in her whole life.

"And you say you saw this man in the Silver Dollar last week?" the sheriff asked Mary.

"The very same. Ain't hard to put two and two together. You got greedy. You pressured Miss Starr, but she wouldn't go along with your demands."

Josie wasn't entirely sure what Mary was talking about, but from the look on the lawman's face, it was clear that he understood all too well.

"So when this other man made her a proposition to let him and his investors set her up in an establishment of her own in Helena, she decided the timing was right. She could get your hands out of her pockets." Mary paused, locking her gaze on the sheriff's pale, watery eyes. After a long moment, he blinked, and she went on. "And put her talents to better use."

The sheriff folded his arms over his chest and leaned back, his wooden chair creaking. "Even if all that's true, why should I believe this man—a man whose name you don't even know—killed James McCumber, when I've got a perfectly good suspect behind bars."

"Because he's a man who'll do anything to get what he wants," Mary replied. "And because you don't want it known that you put so much pressure on a poor working girl that you ran her right out of town."

They were talking about the golden-haired man who'd given her the silver coin, Josie knew, the man Mary thought a killer. Her insides wriggled, and she shoved the handkerchief and coins deep in her pocket. She would have to think long and hard what to do with them.

"So the timing was right for Miss Starr, the Eastern Star," Mary continued. "But the timing was wrong for her brother. He showed up the same day her benefactor drove up from Helena to finalize the deal. The man couldn't count on Miss Starr holding out against her brother's efforts to persuade her. So he removed the obstacle to his plans himself, staging it to look like a roadside robbery. He didn't count on you jumping to the wrong conclusion."

"And you think this big-time businessman from Helena would stoop to murder."

"I think you'll find that knife belonged to him, and that one of his cronies will be all too happy to identify it. Obviously, Miss Starr can tell you his name and where to find him, but if you don't trust her, check the hotel register."

The sheriff gave Mary a long look. Then he reached for the knife and slid it into his desk drawer. He pulled out a ring of keys, stood, and walked slowly to the locked door.

• • •

"Mary! You came." Sarah McCumber, once Miss Starr, never to be the Eastern Star, extended her hands, a beaded reticule hanging from one white-gloved wrist.

Mary took the offered hands in hers and held them tight. "You sure about this, Miss Starr? You swore you weren't never going back."

Behind them in the corral, the stagecoach driver and the undertaker were strapping a pine casket onto the back of the coach bound for Helena, the full-chested black horses waiting patiently.

"I wasn't cruel enough to kill, and I'm not cruel enough to send my brother's body back to our parents by itself." She released her grip and wiped a tear from one powdered cheek. "I'm through with the life, Mary. I enjoyed the freedom it gave me, but it killed my brother."

"Ain't freedom that killed nobody, Miss Starr. It was greed, pure and simple."

"Ready to board, Miss," the driver called, and she nodded her head, then turned back to Mary.

"You tell that little Josie thank you and goodbye for me." She pulled several silver coins from her bag and laid them in Mary's palm. "Give her these. And buy her a peppermint stick."

Mary swallowed hard as the woman who made mourning clothes elegant climbed into the stage and waved goodbye with one gloved hand.

There weren't no telling about people in this world.

COMING CLEAN

Louisine's slender fingers caught in the folds of her long black skirt as she fumbled for the rosary attached to her belt.

"Holy Mary, Mother of God," she muttered, the morning sun streaming through the plain glass windows of the small white church. The other nuns had already left, sweeping out after the last hymn ended. "Pray for us sinners . . ."

Sinners.

She bowed her head, the weight of uncertainty too great. It felt sinful to betray another's secret, especially when speaking up might be seen as petty revenge.

But wasn't it just as wrong to stay silent, when revealing the truth might prevent a greater sin and save a soul?

Even out here in Montana Territory, where the laws of man were often disregarded, the laws of God abided.

Didn't they?

• • •

"I should have listened to my father," Louisine said. "I never should have come West."

"Child, whatever's wrong can't be that bad, can it?" Mary Fields regarded the young woman at her side as they left the church and passed the convent, a low, single-story building the Ursuline Sisters had taken over from the Jesuits when they arrived at St. Peter's Mission to the Blackfeet Indians. The Sisters had come to Montana Territory more than a year and a half ago, in January of the Year of Our Lord 1884. After arriving in the southeastern corner of this vast territory and setting up first a school for white children in Miles City and then a school at the Mission to the Cheyenne at St. Labré, they'd heeded the urgent pleas to come here, to St. Peter's, just as the winter's snows began in earnest. Mary herself had come this past spring, when word that Mother Amadeus was gravely ill had reached the Motherhouse in Toledo. She'd joined Louisine and several other nuns and they made their way West to nurse the woman they all loved. God had blessed their journey, and Amadeus had recovered fully.

Birdsong and human chatter flitted in the distance. Mary didn't bother to attend every service—the nuns and priests prayed enough for the rest of them, and no one seemed to mind her absence. Besides, she had work to do. But she'd been in a thoughtful mood this Sunday morning, so when the bell rang, she'd followed the procession to Mass. From her place in back, she'd seen the troubled look on Louisine's face and when the nun remained alone in prayer, Mary had waited.

Underneath the black veil and white linen, Louisine was a pretty thing who could have married easily back in Ohio. Mary knew that her parents had not been surprised when the youngest of their four girls, born the year the war ended, had chosen the convent. Still, she could well imagine the protests when Louisine announced her decision to join the small band of women traveling West to St. Peter's. Chaperoned, of course, though what they had thought of Mary herself, she had little doubt. "That old Black woman who worked for

Judge Dunne? He kept her out of trouble more than once—she's no fit guide for proper young ladies." Or some such disapproving blather.

But the unlikely crew had made the trip by steamboat, train, and stage without a lick of trouble, thanks in part to the respect given religious women and in part to Mary. Her bulk alone intimidated even most white men, and that was before they knew about the pistol in her pocket.

A young woman on the verge of tears, though, was a different kettle of fish. Mary had seen plenty of fussing in a lifetime of working in white houses, and she didn't much care for it. After the judge's wife died and she took the children to the convent where his sister, Miss Theresa, lived—she never had gotten used to calling that capable woman Mother Amadeus—Mary had seen more than a few novices sent home. Some couldn't give up the comforts of worldly life; others were gently told that perhaps their true vocations lay elsewhere. Louisine, though, had never struck her that way.

"I can't help you," she told the girl, "unless you tell me what's wrong."

"Mary, is there ever good reason to betray another's secret? Something you heard or saw that you shouldn't have?"

"Depends. Did you make a promise? Is someone in danger?"

"No, and maybe." Louisine reached out to finger a wild rose, the fragrant pink flowers long gone, the crimson hips swelling. Soon, the schoolgirls would pluck the hips and they'd be boiled into a syrup used in cough mixtures or to flavor other medicines.

At the sound of clattering wheels, the two women paused to watch a wagon pulling out from behind the barn. Mary recognized Will Hunt, surprised that he wasn't staying for the noon meal with the Jesuits. She hadn't noticed him at Mass. A skilled carpenter, Will lived with his brother Frank and his family on a homestead halfway between the Mission and the town of Cascade. The Hunt brothers had made themselves useful first to the Jesuits, and now to the Ursulines.

Mary turned to ask what new additions to the compound Mother Amadeus was planning, but the look on Louisine's face silenced her.

Her chin set and her jaw tight, the young nun nodded. "Yes. Yes, I think there is danger. I've been praying, but God hasn't told me what to do."

"Then you got to tell Mother Amadeus," Mary said as they resumed their walk. "That woman always knows what to do."

• • •

But Louisine didn't tell Mother Amadeus, not that day. Even Sunday, a day of rest back home, was busy at St. Peter's. The settlers' children had returned, now that the crops were in and the hay put up. The Indian children had their classes, too, and while there was no instruction on the Lord's Day, children had to be minded, prayers said, and meals prepared. The nuns were expected to cook for all the women and girls, and when the settlers came in for Mass, on Sundays and feast days, that could mean a dozen extra mouths at the women's table.

Louisine did her chores with half a mind, and that half asking God to forgive her, if He could not enlighten her.

The next day, Monday, was wash day. Though the skies dawned clear, Louisine's mood grew cloudy. Thank goodness the heat had broken and the work would not be so taxing, though still hot enough and hard enough.

She was paired with Sister Elizabeth for the task, and that brought its own burdens. On the trip West this past spring,

Elizabeth had taken charge, guiding the young Sisters spiritually and physically. She had done well, showing great promise for her future with the order. But since their arrival, Louisine had detected in her friend, just two years older, a restlessness of spirit beyond the eagerness to bring the Word of God to the pagan children of the Great Plains and the Rocky Mountains.

And it had been on that trip that Elizabeth had also discovered Louisine's secret.

But while her own failing was a minor transgression, the other woman's error had led her to the brink of mortal danger. Or so Louisine feared.

She said a quick, silent prayer to Our Lady for guidance, then picked up her heavy serge skirt and stepped through the thick grasses, glad of her sturdy boots. So many unexpected dangers out here. Only a week ago, Mary had killed a snake behind her cabin with the back of a shovel.

The scent of woodsmoke greeted her as she neared the washhouse, newly built this past summer with lumber from a mill she'd visited with Mary. Elizabeth had already set out the tubs and washboards. They would continue working outside while the weather held. Hands on her hips, the other woman surveyed the baskets of black clothing. So much black clothing.

"Good heavens, Sister," Louisine said lightly. "It seems as if the piles grow behind our backs."

"They grow more bountifully than the crops," Elizabeth replied, an edge in her voice that alarmed Louisine. The sisters' duties at the Mission included washing, baking, and mending for the priests, tasks the new arrivals had not anticipated. Louisine suspected Mother Amadeus chafed at them as well, though she had said no such thing to the women.

Elizabeth sprinkled soap powder into a tub of hot water and started on the priests' white collars. Mary rounded the corner with a bucket fresh from the fire, her young black-and-white dog, Jess, beside her. Louisine greeted her friend, then readied a second tub for rinsing and another for the starch. Thank goodness Mother had insisted they buy soap from the mercantile in Cascade rather than spend precious time making their own. And she'd been delighted by the box iron they'd brought from Toledo, quickly grasping how a slug of hot metal inserted into the base of the iron kept it hot longer and the white linen whiter.

Mary returned to her fire, safely away from the wooden building, and the two nuns worked in silence. Louisine ran the collars through the mangle to remove excess water and smooth the fabric, then carried them into the washhouse to dry away from the fine dirt that seemed to cling to everything here.

When she stepped out of the building, she was surprised to see Elizabeth gazing up at the heavens, hands clasped at her breast, washboard forgotten. Trouble emanated from her spirit.

Louisine reached out a hand. "It is not too late to repent, Sister," she said, knowing the moment the words were out that her prayer and her tongue had failed her. Once again, she had spoken with more frankness than humility.

Anger flashed in Elizabeth's brown eyes, then she cast them downward and let out a long, ragged breath. "I would ask how you dare speak to me that way, but I know how you dare. I am a greater sinner than you."

What could she say to that? Vanity and disobedience were a schoolgirl's missteps compared to the terrible secret she feared her friend was keeping. But all sin required confession and penance. "It's not too late," she repeated, dropping her hand and reaching for her rosary. "Confess your shame—"

"I am not ashamed," came the swift reply. "You're not interested in my soul. You're only interested in reclaiming your trifle. You have no trouble breaking your vows, while condemning me for questioning mine."

Shocked, Louisine struggled to calm herself. This was so unlike the Elizabeth she had come to know and admire. But if the woman were only questioning her vows, if she had not yet broken them, then perhaps Louisine could help restore God's peace to her heart.

"I would like the ring back, that's true. It came from my grandmère. You know what it means to me." As the youngest of four girls, she'd had few fine things, and could not bring herself to leave behind the one precious gift she'd received. Instead, she had worn her grandmother's ring on a cord around her neck, managing to keep it hidden for the two years she'd lived at the Motherhouse. But the cramped conditions on their journey had exposed it. Elizabeth had seen, and understood.

Or so Louisine had thought. A few days ago, she'd removed the ring for her bath, wrapped it in a handkerchief, and tucked it in her trunk. When she took advantage of a rare private moment to reclaim her treasure, both handkerchief and ring were gone.

"What if I refuse? You'll tell Mother?" Despite the taunting words, Elizabeth's voice shook and she bit her lower lip. "I'll tell her I spotted one of the women settlers with it after a meal. That I recognized it and took it to force you both to confess your sins."

Louisine stifled a cry. What had gotten into her friend, her traveling companion, her sister in Christ? Bile rose in her throat, hot and sour, and she wanted to retch, but she knew she must remain firm. Compassionate, but resolute.

If Elizabeth told Mother Amadeus about the ring, Louisine would be punished for the breach of her vows. It meant so very much to her, a reminder of the grandmother who had encouraged her devotion to God and of the home she might never see again. She might be allowed to return the ring to her family, rather than watch it be sold to support their work. But at least she would not be countenancing the threat to blame an innocent neighbor.

What had Elizabeth planned to do with the ring? She had not meant to return it or give it to Mother, of that Louisine was certain.

"Sister." She held out her hands, palms up in supplication. "I cannot believe that you, my most loving, generous friend, would blame another for your own wrongdoing if there were not a larger weight upon your mind. Think nothing more about my grandmère's gift. I am willing to bear its loss for your salvation. To save you from sin."

For a moment, it was nearly impossible to believe that the sun still shone, that the meadowlarks still sang and the creek still babbled, so dark and desperate was the look on Elizabeth's face. In the world, she would have been called handsome, her features strong and even, her gaze intense but pleasant. But none of that was visible now. All Louisine could see was anguish and despair.

"Is it too much?" she asked her friend, keeping her voice quiet, concerned. "We work hard here, harder than I ever imagined. But we must do it, to build a better life for the children, and for God."

Elizabeth did not reply.

"Are you sorry you came?" Louisine said. "One of the priests is returning to seminary. Maybe he could escort you—"

"No!" Elizabeth raised her head, eyes flashing. "I'm not sorry. If I hadn't come, I would never—"

She broke off and Louisine's heart sank. It was as she had feared. She took a step closer. "Let me help you. Let us pray for God's strength, so you can resist the temptations of the flesh."

"Oh, it is worse than that, my friend," the other woman said. "I do not want to resist them. I have told God one thing, but my heart tells me another."

That meant, then, that she had not yet given in to desire. That there might be hope. Not that Louisine believed intimacy wrong. Not at all. Her two oldest sisters were married, with children, and though they said little about the marriage bed, it was clear that they were happy in their lives.

She and Elizabeth had chosen God and professed their vows. Renouncing those vows was not impossible. But it would be a scandal, here and in Toledo. The taint would follow Elizabeth wherever she went.

"Have you spoken to Mother? Told her of your—feelings?"

"What could she say, little sister? What could she do? Other than banish me to the church and implore me to pray?" She shook her head. "I am done with prayer. It has done nothing for me."

And with that, she wiped her damp palms on her skirt, lifted it, and ran down the hill toward Birch Creek.

• • •

Mary put out a hand to stop the dog in his tracks and leaned against the side of the washhouse, water sloshing from her bucket. Though she'd heard only fragments of the conversation between the two young nuns, the tone was clear. It had been pained and fervent. She could only guess at the trouble between them. Louisine had a good heart and a quick mind—this past June, she'd helped Mary think up a plan to aid the pregnant half-breed wife of an indifferent white cattleman and their daughter, and persuaded Mother Amadeus to go along. Alas, by the time they'd put their plan in motion, the woman and baby had died, but the girl, Josie, was now thriving in the nuns' care.

Elizabeth, though, had undergone a change since they'd reached the territory last spring. The group had been scheduled to travel West later, after the weather improved, but when the telegram came to say that Amadeus was deathly ill with pneumonia, Mary had sworn to make the trip right then, telling the Mother Superior she could send the young nuns with her now or let them find their own way in another month. Two days later, the group had caught the train in Toledo.

Their arrival had been an answer to many prayers. Mary had nursed Amadeus back to health and stayed. Not everyone approved. But Mary had decided long ago to never mind what others thought of her, as long as she could earn her way in the world. A remnant of her childhood when all around her people were bought and sold, families separated without a word or a care.

During the trip, it had been Elizabeth who reminded them of the hours for prayer, who blessed their food and asked God to keep them safe, to give them strength for the journey and the challenges ahead. She had calmed her sisters' fears and swept away the taunts a crude man lobbed at them when they changed trains, making the sign of the cross in his direction with a graceful hand. When strangers asked about their journey, she'd answered with generosity and inquired about their travels in return. She'd not been as cheery or chatty as Louisine—of all the good Lord's creatures, only the chickadees could outtalk that one.

But since midsummer, something had been amiss. Mary

had often spotted Elizabeth staring at nothing, her expression more troubled than reverent, and this was not the first time Mary had heard her speak harshly to Louisine, though on the journey, they had seemed fast friends.

Amadeus had noticed the changes, Mary was sure. When it came to the sisters, Mother Amadeus saw everything. But she'd been distracted lately by the needs of the children—far greater than they had expected—and the urgent need to expand and improve the facilities. It seemed to Mary that the Jesuit fathers had placed a greater burden on the women than they had a right to do. But then, men often did.

She cocked her head, sure she heard Louisine sobbing. Elizabeth had nearly reached the creek. The leaves of the chokecherries and other wild shrubs were beginning to yellow but still provided dense cover in which to hide. To sit in prayer or thought, or conversation.

If she gathered right, Elizabeth had taken something Louisine valued, but Louisine was more worried about her friend than the object. Mary knew too little of the theft to tell the sheriff, even if she did trust the man.

When it came to trouble and temptation, life in Montana Territory wasn't much different from Ohio. Sins of the flesh and the spirit could be found anywhere.

And talking to Amadeus would only stir the pot.

Mary put a hand to her low back and stretched. The country was growing on her, but it wasn't easy land. What would winter be like?

The bucket of hot water was getting heavier and colder.

"Come on with you, Jess," she called, more to alert Louisine than to summon the dog. It didn't do to startle people when they were suffering.

• • •

Her whiskey jug was nearly dry by the next Saturday when Mary drove the wagon into Cascade to collect the sisters' mail and supplies. The sky was clear, stretched wide above the horizon, and she slowed near Square Butte to watch the meadowlarks play. They flew high, waited for the wind, then fluttered near to the ground before swooping out and flying straight up, ready to ride again. Not a care in the world.

"Fool birds," she muttered to Jess beside her on the wagon seat and gave the reins a little snap to urge the horses along.

In Cascade, a dusty town on the west bank of the Missouri River, she drove to the stables, unhitched the pair and wiped them down, then headed for the general store that also served as the post office. On the corner where the main streets met, two men emerged from the bank and paused on the steps. The banker, belly stretching his vest and watch chain, said a few words, then held out his hand to the other man. *Will Hunt.* Hunt shook the banker's hand, then bounded into the street. A wagon rattling down the hill made a too-wide turn and both driver and banker shouted. Hunt's head jerked up and he staggered backward, hat flying, just managing to avoid being run over. By the time the wagon passed and Mary caught sight of him again, he'd picked up his hat and stood on the corner, dusting it off.

She shook her head and ambled on.

"Mary," Mr. Whitney, the shopkeeper, said when she entered the Mercantile, her next stop. "Fine day for a drive."

She allowed that it was. Several packages for the Mission had arrived, and they agreed that he'd put them out front, ready to load into her wagon on her way out of town. She handed over her list. He was good to the sisters, but why wouldn't he be? Unlike some, Mother Amadeus paid their accounts on time. Mary turned to leave. The door opened and Will Hunt stepped in from the boardwalk, looking no worse for the wear.

"Mary," he said, hand moving instinctively to his hat, though he didn't remove it. She nodded in acknowledgment, and paused near the notions display, pretending to examine the buttons. Something about Hunt seemed different today, from his glad-handed way of taking leave of the banker to his carelessness of the wagon and now his low conversation with the shopkeeper. They weren't passing time jawing about the weather, or looking over a list of supplies. The shopkeeper raised a finger and stepped into the back room. A moment later, he returned, a brown paper bundle tied with string in his hands. He set the bundle down, then drew out the account book.

Mary couldn't hear the figure the shopkeeper named. Hunt pulled out a clip of paper money and peeled off several bills. The two men shook hands across the counter.

"Good luck to you, then," the shopkeeper called as Hunt picked up the parcel and strode past her.

Mary stayed put, pondering. Not that there was anything suspicious about the transaction, but most people bought their goods on account and paid once a month with a bank draft. What was in the parcel? And why had the shopkeeper wished Hunt good luck? That suggested a change of some kind, didn't it?

"Something I can help you with, Mary?" the shopkeeper asked.

She waved a hand and headed for the door. This was a mystery better contemplated over whiskey.

• • •

Mary was sitting on her usual stool at the far end of the Silver Dollar's well-polished bar, three sips into a glass of rye, when

Will Hunt arrived. If he saw her, he didn't let on. Mary was the only woman the barkeeper allowed to drink in here, though she allowed as how she was probably the only one who wanted to. And she gave good business, always filling her jug for the dry spells between trips to town.

Folks in and around Cascade tolerated her just fine. A handful of Black cowboys roamed the range, and she'd heard of a few colored families in the territory, but far as she knew, she was the only Black woman around on her own. Tolerated or not, she almost never presumed to speak with someone who didn't start the conversation. But taking care to observe the distances other people kept from her didn't mean she couldn't listen.

And Mary heard all kinds of talk—plenty of folks who wouldn't say more than "'morning, Mary" to her had no qualms speaking freely within earshot. As if by ignoring her presence, they closed her ears.

But her sharp ears did her little good at the moment. She watched in the mirror as Will Hunt took a seat on the far side of the room with two men who ran cattle east of the river. She didn't get the impression he had much to say. It was almost as if he'd deliberately sat as far from her as he could and stay inside the saloon's four walls. He downed his whiskey and stood, the other men pushing back their chairs to stand and shake his hand.

Will Hunt sure was doing a lot of handshaking today.

"You'll be missed," she heard one of the other men say, his voice carrying. "But there is better work farther west—you're right about that."

Well, I'll be, she said to herself. Not what she'd expected at all.

Not at all.

• • •

Mary put the matter of Will Hunt out of mind. An old woman's foolishness, nothing more. Though the weather held, in that way that sometimes convinced you it would stay fine and never change, she knew better. She talked one of the young priests into letting her borrow a pair of older boys and supervised as they rebuilt the wall of the chicken coop where the fox had clawed the boards loose, and put a sturdy fence around the chicken yard. After that, she set them to splitting a pile of wood stashed behind her cabin. A woman came in to help put up the wild plums and ready the last of the garden produce for the root cellar, and Mary was pressed into service along with the older girls. Not that she minded—she was as fond of food as anyone else and had no intention of dying of starvation when the snow fell.

Outside of Mass, she caught only fleeting glimpses of Louisine, looking pale and thin. Mary considered talking to Mother Amadeus. But the woman had worry enough without Mary bringing her troubles born of little more than imagination. Amadeus was a woman of God, but she kept a firm hand on matters of this world as well. There had been a flurry of letters between her and the bishops in Helena and Toledo, no doubt about the school, the progress of the Indian children, even the demands of the priests. The Jesuits had promised the Ursulines control of the Mission, but it appeared to Mary that they had kept their word only in that they did not interfere with the schooling of the Indian girls. In everything else, from insisting that the women run a separate school for the settlers' daughters, to a say in construction, to the ever-annoying laundry and mending, the men maintained the upper hand.

And Mary figured that suited Amadeus about as well as it would have suited her. Which was to say, not one whit.

Construction had begun on the new dormitory, and

though Mary saw Frank Hunt several times, she caught no sign of his brother.

Then one morning, a week or so after the spat between the two young nuns, Mary was talking to her hens and snatching their eggs out from under them when she heard a commotion outside the coop.

"Where's that fool dog of mine?" she muttered. "He's supposed to keep the foxes away and the roosters in his sights."

But the flutter was of serge skirts, not roosters' wings.

"Mary," Louisine said, clutching her skirt with one hand, eyes wide, her color high. "She's gone. Not a word to anyone. She's gone."

"Child, what are you on about?" But Mary could feel her own heart begin to tremble.

"Come with me. To the dormitory. Before Mother sees."

Mary glanced up at the sun. Amadeus would be deep in morning prayer. Where Louisine ought to be. She hung her basket on a fence post and the two women walked across the field.

"If she . . ." Louisine said, not finishing the thought. "I couldn't live with myself if . . ."

Mary wanted to say that she'd be surprised what she could live with, but the girl was too wrecked.

The nuns slept in a small room at the far end of the dormitory. At the foot of each narrow bed stood a traveling trunk, large enough to hold an extra habit and spare linen, and a few books. On top of one trunk was a pile of neatly folded clothing—habit, veil, and white collar.

Mary stared, out of breath, willing herself to comprehend.

"And this," Louisine said. "She left this." From beneath the pile, she withdrew a cream-colored envelope. The envelope was blank.

Mary took it and pulled out the single page inside and read slowly.

I can no longer live the vows I have taken. Though I know my actions will cause great sorrow, blame no one but me. If I must live under the control of men, I would rather it be a man I love and admire, who will make it his mission, his vow, to care for me. I am sorry I could not live up to your faith in me.

Something more lay inside the envelope. Mary shook it into her palm—a small gold ring with a touch of filigree. Beside her, Louisine gasped. Mary did not bother to ask where Elizabeth had obtained the ring—the girl's reaction made clear that it was hers. Mary closed her thick fingers over the ring and shoved her hand in her pocket. If, indeed, Elizabeth had fled the Mission, alone or with Will Hunt, Amadeus would be distraught. Mary could see no reason to upset her further by revealing that Louisine had kept an item which was forbidden to her, or that Elizabeth had stolen it to keep the younger nun quiet.

Surely that was the reason for the theft. Elizabeth could have sold the ring to pay her way. That she had not done so suggested that someone else had helped her leave and would be helping her build a new life in the world.

And it suggested that Elizabeth was attempting to buy Louisine's silence even after her departure.

No, Mary thought, as she read the letter again. Whatever her sins, Elizabeth had known it would be wrong to take the ring, one final breach of duty to God and her sisters.

Elizabeth's actions would have repercussions for them all. But Mary would not force Louisine into the sin of disobeying Mother Amadeus when she demanded, as was her right and her obligation, to hear all that Louisine knew of Elizabeth's departure and plans. Mary, on the other hand, had taken no such vow.

Those demands would be made soon, if the approaching footsteps were any indication.

Amadeus needed only a glance to grasp the situation. She fell to her knees, crossed herself, and began uttering low, rapid pleas to God above.

At last, Amadeus stood. Mary handed her the letter and she read, then turned her attention to Louisine. "And you knew nothing of this?"

The young nun shook her head. "I—I knew she was troubled, Mother, but—"

"We all knew, child." Amadeus reached unsteadily behind her for Elizabeth's bed and sat. "I failed her."

"Miss Theresa, you did no such thing," Mary said.

"Mary. For once, hold your tongue."

The words should have stung, but didn't. What stung was the knowledge that she could do nothing to lift the woman's pain. Amadeus saw each of the nuns as her charge. Her responsibility. How much she guessed of Louisine's complicity, Mary had no idea.

Guilt and anguish had sucked the air from the room, and Mary swayed from side to side. *What was that, under the bed?* She bent down and drew out a length of brown paper and a string.

She recalled the package Will Hunt had picked up at the Mercantile. Traveling clothes for Elizabeth, she reckoned now, with a glance at the trunk and the abandoned habit.

"So she is safe," Amadeus said, the relief of that knowledge barely softening the pain in her voice. "But where could she have gone?"

That, no one knew.

The next day, Frank Hunt confirmed that his brother had

left the area, and Mary watched as Amadeus suffered with the knowledge that Will and Elizabeth must have left together. A lesser woman might have felt betrayed. Amadeus, though, blamed herself. She had been too busy, too distracted to truly understand the pain and conflict Elizabeth had been experiencing. Had the hard life here and the realization that the women would never be wholly in charge made the young nun vulnerable to the longing in a kind man's eyes? To a yearning, perhaps a love, she had promised to leave behind?

The sisters put it about that Elizabeth had traveled east with the departing Jesuit, returning to Toledo to assist her ailing father. Mary could see what the lie cost Amadeus, but she well understood that silence was their only security. Amadeus and Louisine spent countless hours in the church, praying to those sinners who knew the temptations of the flesh: Mary Magdalene, St. Augustine, Mary of Egypt.

Mary Fields of St. Peter's Mission prayed only that the prayers would heal her old friend, whose heart, she knew, was more than a little broken.

• • •

A few days after Elizabeth's disappearance, Mary sat on the porch of her cabin, soaking her feet in the washtub. Beside her, Jess raised his head as Louisine came into view.

"Sit you down. You got a look that worries me."

Louisine sat, her hands in her lap. "I came to thank you for not telling Mother Amadeus about the ring."

"What good would that do?" Mary replied. "I'll hold on to it until you need it. Maybe someday you'll be in charge here and you can decide then whether to enjoy a bit of beauty, or sell it to buy sewing thread and school books."

"You lied for me," Louisine pressed.

"I didn't lie for nobody." The water had cooled and Mary's wooden chair creaked as she shifted her weight to lift out one big, reddened foot. "Wouldn't never. Just didn't tell her what I didn't think she needed to know. She's got sorrow enough."

"But God sees. He knows."

"Child, it's past time for you to forgive yourself. Keeping a trinket won't keep you out of heaven. And you couldn't have told Mother about the theft without revealing your fears for Sister Elizabeth. Or whatever she's calling herself now."

"I put my concerns for myself first."

Mary ran a rough towel over her wet foot. "Don't know as how we can blame ourselves for not speaking up. Elizabeth had to deal with her troubles in her own way."

"Do you think they'll be happy?"

"In time," Mary replied. "Once she forgives herself." Because the real sin, Mary knew in her heart, was to fail to see God in ourselves and in each other, in the meadowlarks at play, in the wild roses, and in the creek as it rolled on by.

A BITTER WIND

November, 1914

Thomas Whitney flinched against the cold, sharp snow that bit his face and stung his eyes. Now that he was a grown man with a wife and children, he understood why folks in Montana complained about the weather. He supposed people elsewhere were just as preoccupied with it, especially men who worked the land or the rails. Women, too—the farm and ranch wives, and any woman who'd lost half her flock to a sudden freeze or seen a garden flattened by a late-afternoon hailstorm.

If you had people you worried about protecting, storms didn't blow over quite so quick.

When it came to work, he'd been lucky, though keeping shop hadn't been what he'd set out to do. He'd lived his whole life within thirty miles of Cascade, not counting a few months laying stone at mission schools around the state, but he sure wouldn't mind if the fool wind took a liking to another clime now and then and moved on.

Ahead of him, young Thomas—Tommy—steered the wheelbarrow of firewood up the path. He'd overloaded it, despite his father's caution, and keeping it moving forward took all the muscle the twelve-year-old had. He'd learn. The boy was smart, like his mother, and willing to work hard. Thomas gave himself some credit for that.

The neighbor's small white house was not so tidy as usual, though the townspeople had repaired the damage caused by the fire in the laundry, and Mary had continued taking in wash until recently. Nothing was tidy, this time of year. The lace curtains were closed, a small blue jelly jar on the windowsill. He caught no whiff of smoke and saw none rising from the chimney. They'd fix that soon enough, getting a fire crackling in the cookstove hot enough to warm the two-room house. Then they'd heat up the kettle of soup nestled in the wooden bucket he carried in his good hand, to warm up his neighbor's old bones. Her favorite—split pea with leftover ham. The fragrance coming off the kettle made his mouth water, even though he'd already had a full meal.

"Pa, look." The barrow staggered to a halt as Tommy pointed at a bush in the front garden, poking out of its bed of snow. Frost rimed the deep green leaves and the single rose, the pink-and-white petals almost striped. "How can it be blooming so late in the year, with the snow and all? Everything else is frozen dead."

"Mary always did have a way with flowers," Thomas told his son. Hollyhocks and delphinium, iris, phlox, and peonies. Mary rarely showed up for a gathering without a bouquet in hand, whether it was a birthday celebration or a wedding. Or a funeral.

But this rose. Still in bloom despite the wind, despite the cold. Despite the years and the hard way it had come to be here. He thought about that day out on the Mission Road, at the homestead south of Fishback Butte. When he'd seen Mary Fields size things up and do what was needed, even summoning help from a man who had no reason to want to give it. Mary was a woman you wanted to do things for.

"She's old," the boy said. "Ain't nobody else as old as she is around here. Ain't nobody else Black."

"Isn't," Thomas corrected, the way his wife always did. Once a schoolteacher . . . "She is old and she's been good to us. Biggest heart I ever knew, but even a big heart gives out when the time comes. So you remember to keep an eye on her and make sure she's taken care of."

"Like we're doing now."

"That's right. Like my uncle used to say, when you run the general store, keeping an eye on folks is part of the job." Thomas stepped onto the porch and raised his hand to knock. The left hand, the one that never had healed properly. Another gust struck his face. He glanced down at the rose one more time. It took him back, it did.

• • •

May, 1897

Mary Fields drew her team to a halt in front of the town stables. Arched her spine, the reins loose in one hand. On the seat beside her, Jess pushed himself up onto his front paws, his black nose in the air, the funny way dogs did.

"Ain't so easy getting old, is it, Jess?" she asked. "But there ain't no use complaining. We got a good roof over our heads and decent work to put food on the table. Or in the bowl." She chuckled. Folks said she spoiled him, but it wasn't nothing more than he deserved. Not after putting up with her all these years.

For the past two years, she'd been an official postal driver, carrying the mail out to St. Peter's Mission, stopping at the homesteads along the way. Saturdays, like today, she delivered freight and grocery orders, too. Pretty drive this time of year, early May, the bluebells and tiny white ground phlox poking up, the fields beginning to come to life. Ever since the winter of '86–'87, more and more ranchers had been fencing their cattle and putting up hay against another terrible tragedy. That had been her second winter in the territory, so bitter cold it was frozen in the memories of everyone who'd survived it—and even some who hadn't come here yet. Cows had disappeared in the snow drifts and so had the cowhands who went after them. She was no fan of Charlie Russell, not after his drawing of the town showed her sitting on her behind in the middle of the road with her basket of eggs all broken, but his sketch of the starving cow, the one that made him a famous artist, had it about right. They'd been finding the bones well into the next spring.

Now she'd been in Montana a full dozen years, since before statehood, and the land still took her by surprise. Harsh, but beautiful, in a surprising way. Nothing like Tennessee, a place she missed only in her fever dreams.

Never did her no good to go back there in her mind, to where she'd been born and reared. She pushed the thought away.

Extra load today. What manner of woman she was waiting on, Mary didn't know. Some females were interesting; others made a twelve-mile drive feel like thirty, Mary trying to keep her eyes open and her ears shut. Not that she had reason to worry about keeping to the road. Her team, one gray, one chestnut, knew it as well as she did.

Jess sat up, training his rheumy eyes on a movement in the distance. The stage that ran from Fort Benton to Helena. A proper stage, unlike her open wagon, though the wagon had given her the nickname "Stagecoach Mary." After she'd left the Mission, after her restaurant failed, when Mother Amadeus arranged for her to get the postal route, the postmaster down in Helena had done some asking around. Said she was the first colored woman in the country to drive a Star Route. Maybe they'd put her on a stamp someday, she'd joked. Maybe so, he'd replied, looking like he half believed it.

Men.

Mary bunched up her full black skirt and climbed down, her hand going to her right hip, fingers working the flesh along her spine. Arthritis, bursitis, some itis. Didn't matter what you called it—it pained her. She turned to see if the dog needed any help but he'd jumped down on his own, the excitement of the stage's approach making him forget for a moment that he had the itis, too.

"Sit, Jess," she said. No need. Dog had all but trained himself, perched next to her all formal in his black-and-white sheepdog fur like he was somebody's butler. The tips of her fingers grazed the top of his big head.

The stage slowed as it neared the stables. She could tell who was driving from half a mile away, by how the horses carried themselves and the clop of their hooves, how the stage wobbled or hugged the road.

She leaned against the sideboard, arms crossed.

The driver tightened the reins and shouted, as if his horses—a four-horse team—hadn't already shortened their stride and prepared to stop. He was a burly man, as wide as Mary and only a hair taller, his tan hat caked with dust. He scowled at the sight of her and gave the reins an unnecessary tug.

"You stopping a while?" the stable master called as he approached. Behind him came a boy toting two buckets of water. "Rest those horses?"

"They can rest while we do our business. I got to be

getting on to Helena." The driver waved him off, gripping the leather coach strap as he lowered himself, his knees bowing east and west like a drunken sailor. When both feet had touched down, he grunted. Huffed for a moment, then grabbed a wooden box from underneath the seat and set it on the ground. He tugged at his coat, then opened the coach door. Held out a hand. A woman's hand appeared, ungloved, and settled firmly in his, the sleeve of the linen duster riding up as the woman descended to reveal a slender wrist, a white cuff, and a blue jacket sleeve.

It was the blue of a western sky on a fair day, the blue that pierced Mary's heart every time she strode out into it. The blue that filled her lungs almost to bursting, that made the meadowlarks soar and dive as they played on the winds.

A curious choice, under the circumstances. Or maybe not. The color of a last chance?

The woman set one black-booted foot on the box, then stepped to the ground and shook herself slightly, as if to settle all the pieces back in place. Then she slipped off the duster, revealing a blue traveling skirt and a short jacket trimmed with black braid. A small cloth purse hung from her belt.

"Thank you kindly," she said and handed the driver the duster, her voice soft but warm, tinged with a faint eastern accent Mary couldn't identify.

She was young, no more than twenty, her profile strong, her hat dark green. She scanned her surroundings, her gaze slow and steady, like the river. From here, you could see across the Missouri, high with late-spring runoff, not so wide as downstream. When she came to Mary, waiting beside the wagon, she paused, then continued on, taking in the town. What there was of it. Dusty dirt roads. A mix of frame and sandstone buildings—the bank, the general store, the jail, a saloon. Town had grown a lot since Mary's arrival twelve years ago, especially since the bridge went up a few years back.

The driver tossed the duster onto the seat. Then he reached into the coach and hauled out a carpetbag, the pattern a swirl of red, green, and brown, grunting again as he set it down. The woman pointed, saying something Mary couldn't hear. The twitch of the man's shoulders telegraphed his displeasure as he reached inside the coach a second time. Came out with a metal can, clearly heavy. The woman cradled it in both arms. She smiled, though the driver's frown remained unchanged.

The stable master gave a little bow. "Welcome to Cascade, Miss—"

"Morgan. Amelia Morgan, from western Pennsylvania."

"You've come a long ways," he said. "Though we've got folks from all over around here. Don't we, Mary? Mary drives the postal route west of town. Knows just about everybody. She'll take you out to the Mission." He gestured toward Mary and the wagon.

Mary was still turning the woman's name over in her mind. Thought she ought to be able to place it, though the note asking that she pick up the passenger hadn't given a name.

If Miss Amelia Morgan was surprised to be met by a woman, and a big Black woman at that, she hid it well. Instead, she shifted the can to her hip, encircling it with her arm, and reached out to scratch behind Jess's ear.

"We had a dog like him on the farm. Better at scattering the sheep and chickens than herding them, but a sweet boy."

"Name's Jess," Mary said. "And he never yet met a chicken he didn't want to eat. Though he's smart enough to figure out it's best to let them be."

"Good Jess," the new arrival said. Her eyes were as deep brown and intense as the dog's, a bit of lace and dark green ribbon at the collar of her white blouse. A dark curl strayed from under her hat, the only sign of the strain of travel.

"Can we find a safe place for this?" Amelia said, nodding at the can. It was filled with dirt, a few green stalks poking out, tight clusters of leaves at their tips.

"Yes'm, I'm sure we can," Mary said. A rose, by the look of it. Foolish bit of sentiment, maybe, though she hardly blamed the woman. But what did she expect to do with it out here?

The stable master picked up the carpetbag, its weight surprising him. "What you got in here? Bricks?"

"Books," Amelia Morgan said. She had one of those faces that seemed plain until she smiled, when all her features lit up from inside.

He hoisted the carpetbag into the rear of the wagon, then returned to the stage to help the driver with the trunk. The two women watched the men wrestle it into place alongside the day's freight and the mailbag. When Mary made no effort to grab the outgoing mail, the coach driver threw her a dark look and grabbed the bag himself, muttering as he hauled it over to the stage and heaved it onto the seat.

If he wanted her to help him, he ought to have been nicer to her all these years, instead of telling tales up and down the stage line. Saying she'd as soon shoot a white man as wish him a good day. That she was a drunk. That the sisters should have sent her away from the Mission a long time ago.

The driver climbed back up and snapped his reins, and the team carried the coach out of town, south toward the capital city.

"I got no patience for a man who don't take care of his animals," she said, "no matter what color his skin is."

"The boy gave his horses a good drink," the stable master said. "They weren't winded. You know I'd have insisted he give them a rest, if I thought they needed it."

"Hmmph," was all she said. It was an old conversation between them, but she and the stable master trusted each other, and she knew he put the horses' care first. Her pair was well-rested and watered, ready for the trip out to the Mission.

"Best be gettin' going." She slapped her thigh. Jess hopped up, using the running board to give himself a boost, and took his place on the wagon seat.

Amelia glanced from Mary to the stable master, then followed him around the wagon to the other side, clutching the can.

"Road's a bit bumpy," Mary said. "Tuck it between your feet and squeeze her tight."

Amelia nodded, looking amused, and set the plant on the floorboard. The stable master held out a hand but she ignored it, hitching up her skirt and grabbing the wagon rail, then hoisting herself up. If she noticed the rifle tucked behind Mary's feet, she did not remark on it. She adjusted the blanket padding the seat and settled herself. Placed one foot on either side of the can.

"Thank you," she said to the man still standing beside the wagon. "I'm sure we'll meet again."

"It'll be my pleasure. Mary and the sisters will take good care of you until . . ." His voice trailed off.

"Until the wedding," Amelia Morgan said. "When I become someone else."

• • •

"Oh, child," Mary said after they'd left the town behind and headed west up the long sloping bench, away from the river.

No point trying to stop herself from laughing. "You had me fooled. The sisters sent a note about a female passenger from back East who needed bringing out to the Mission. I thought you was joining up, and when I saw you climb down from that coach, I told myself 'good, she got some use outta that pretty blue suit before it gets made over for some local woman needing a Sunday best.' Never imagined you were coming out here to get married!"

"Joining up?" Amelia said. "And what do you mean, the Mission? Aren't we going to the hotel? Although I confess, I thought it would be in town, not out here in—" She waved a hand at the broad, open land, dotted with clusters of trees and rock outcroppings. "In all this spaciousness."

"Hotel is full," Mary said, holding the reins in both hands. "Boardinghouse is men only. I'm taking you to St. Peter's Mission. Founded by the Jesuit fathers, to bring salvation to the Indians and teach the boys, though word is they're pulling out. Losing their government money, I expect. The Ursuline Sisters been teaching the girls—the Indians who board and some white girls from the ranch and homestead families. Now they'll teach the boys, too, what's left of 'em."

The road, a pair of tracks pounded across the tall grass prairie by hooves and rutted by wheels, had leveled out. Jess stood up on the seat, made a full circle, and settled back down, his tail thwacking Mary's arm.

"You old dog," she muttered, giving his back a quick pat. "The sisters have two novices right now, and I expected you'd be making a third. If I didn't know better when I saw your traveling outfit, I shoulda figured when I saw that rose."

"It's—it's from the farm," Amelia said, a slight tremble in her voice. "I wanted to bring something of it with me, for the new homestead."

What the land was like in western Pennsylvania, Mary

didn't know. But she knew northern Ohio, with its green, rolling hills. Farmland so rich you could smell it, watered by rippling streams and dotted with cool, leafy forests.

Nothing like this.

"So who you fixin' to marry?" Plenty of single and widowed men around, but Mary hadn't heard a whisper of a wedding.

"George Reynolds. I expect you know him."

"Reynolds. He the fellow come down from near Great Falls, this past spring?" That's why she knew Amelia's name. From the letters.

"Yes. He's tried his hand at a number of ventures since he came West, looking for the right fit. So many possibilities. I finally agreed to marry him when he got the farm, and he sent me the railroad ticket." She blushed beneath the hat. "He says that's why he was so determined to get a place of his own. Of our own."

Mary had seen Reynolds in the general store when she was picking up the mail and her groceries. Tall, dark-haired man, maybe twenty-eight or so, if she remembered right. He'd given her a long look, as many did the first time they saw her. More than a few colored men rode the range, and the Colored Troops of the 10th Cavalry, the Buffalo Soldiers, had been stationed over at Fort Shaw for a while. A good number of families had settled in Fort Benton, Helena, and now Great Falls, the young city downriver from Cascade. But a colored woman on her own was a rare sight.

All she knew about him, if she had the right story for the right man, was that he'd taken over Joe Bergen's place. The Bergen brothers had staked adjacent claims, long since proved up, but Joe Bergen had sold his a month or two past. Why he had sold and where he'd taken himself, no one seemed to agree.

Odd. But then, folks did odd things.

"George came from two towns over," Amelia said. "He wrote home, saying he needed a wife. The letter got to our minister, and he thought of me."

Mary gave her passenger a quick glance. Why was this young woman, not a beauty but clearly with some spunk, willing to come all the way out here to marry? For love, or those possibilities? She let her questions go unasked.

Sometimes, the best way to get people to talk was to hold your tongue and let them fill in the silence.

"Actually, that's not quite true," Amelia said, shifting on the seat and running her hands toward her knees. "The reverend had my older sister in mind, but my father wouldn't hear of it. She is—she is good at taking care of him, far better than I. She could not be spared."

Mary felt her jaw tighten. It always did when she thought about the ways men used their power over women's lives.

"And so when George wrote to her, I replied," Amelia continued. "He came back to be introduced. He has no people left at home—he and his brother have been on their own since they were young. When he returned to Montana, we kept writing. You can tell a lot about a person by their correspondence, don't you think?"

Mary made a living delivering mail and goods, and she had learned to read and write, but letters of her own were scarce.

"Your mother must take it hard, to see you leave," she said.

"My mother and my younger brother died two years ago, when the flu gripped the county. Farming's been difficult ever since the Panic hit in '93, and their passing hit my father hard. My oldest sister and her husband took over. When you farm, you may not have two nickels to rub together, but at least you know you can always eat. But they have seven children and . . ."

Her voice trailed off, the liveliness Mary had heard fading. Was there more to the story than the girl was telling?

"And there wasn't room for you," Mary said.

"After the first two girls, we were all supposed to be the boy. I'm the last of the five sisters." Amelia's voice broke. "Our brother finally came along four years after me. He was worth waiting for."

"That's a lot of loss. My condolences."

"Thank you."

The road followed the rising curve of the land, the horizon changing at every turn.

"I will say I was impressed by the town of Great Falls," Amelia said, the brightness returning. "While I was waiting for the stage, I walked along the river and had a cup of tea in a hotel as grand as any I've seen."

"The Park Hotel," Mary said, knowing the sprawling brick building by sight. "Mr. Gibson built it. Mr. Gibson built pretty near the whole town. Bit of a set-to when the new county was established a few years ago, over whether Cascade or Great Falls should be the county seat. He won."

"Money gets what it wants," Amelia said, though her voice held no bitterness.

They drove on, Amelia studying the countryside.

"Back home," she said, "we'd have passed two townships and half a dozen farms by now. This land is so—I don't want to say barren, but it is different. On the train, it seemed like every mile farther west we went, the farther apart things got. Towns, farms, even the trees. Like giant hands grabbed the land and stretched it out. Makes you feel small, in a way. East of the Mississippi, it's full spring, but the season's just starting out here, isn't it?" She pointed at a buck loping toward a draw. "Even the deer are bigger. You know, I had never seen an antelope until yesterday."

"You'll see plenty," Mary said. "Even eat a few." A jackrabbit darted across the road, the horses not missing a step. A raven cawed. Mary pointed out a fox den in a sage-covered hillock. She told the names of the flat-topped buttes that broke the horizon and cautioned the girl about rattlesnakes. A few years back, when she'd had to shelter in the wagon during a blizzard, Mary had held off wolves with her rifle. She'd seen grizzly bears, and felt the ripple up and down her spine at the cries of a pack of coyotes. She could handle just about anything, but she could not abide snakes.

Eventually, they crossed Lepley Creek, followed the road north, then drove west again. They'd made half a dozen deliveries and Mary had introduced Amelia to one young farm wife and an old bachelor, when they reached a turnout, a thicket of red bark willow along one side. Mary slowed the horses.

"Is this it?" Amelia asked. "The road to my future home?"

Mary nodded. "Road runs along the section line. Splits just over the ridge. You'll be to the west." She raised the reins.

"Can't we stop?"

"I got a schedule to keep."

"Mary, please. George and I are engaged to be married. I don't think he'll be home, but if he is and if I need a chaperone, you're here. Besides, don't the horses need water? Don't we?"

What harm could come from it? She had to admit, she was curious. Like others with cabins and houses a good distance back, the Bergens kept a box for deliveries along the road, though they didn't get much mail. She hadn't seen their homes.

"I s'pose it won't hurt nothing. Heed you now, Paul," she called to the gray. "Come along, Peter." A few minutes later, they crested the ridge and came to a fork in the road. Not that it was much of a road, just two rutted tracks, the right clearly more used. Mary kept to the left. After another quarter of a mile, the homestead came into view. An unpainted cabin, boards darkened by the sun, a porch running along the front. A bachelor's cabin, most likely the original homestead, a root cellar beneath and a privy out back. More substantial than some Mary had seen. When she'd first arrived, a sod roof had been a common sight.

A two-story addition had been roughed in above a stone foundation. A stack of lumber fresh from the mill stood off to the side, a long ladder leaning against it. A few scrubby pines clustered behind the buildings, and the land sloped down to a brushy stretch where the stream ran.

"Oh," Amelia said, the single syllable buoyed with expectation and burdened by uncertainty.

No smoke rose from the chimney. No horse grazed nearby. Beside the cabin lay a large garden, a walking plow parked at the edge as though someone had thought about planting, then thought again. To the west stood a small hay shed, well-weathered, and a corral, the rail fence so freshly hewn that the breeze carried a hint of pine. A cow lowed and came into view, a calf trailing behind her.

Despite her suit and hat, Amelia was a farm girl. She'd know what to do with the livestock, and how to raise vegetables and put them up.

"He saved the calf," Amelia said, clapping her hands together. "He was worried. It's the cow's first, and he sat up all night with them while they figured out cleaning and suckling." She climbed down from the wagon and headed for the corral. Jess bounded after her.

Mary set the wagon's brake. "Traitor," she muttered, and lowered herself to the ground. Reached into the bed for the bucket. Next to it sat the carpetbag, heavy with books and the things Amelia had needed for the journey. Was this truly the life she wanted? It was a rare woman who got to choose.

No point unhitching the team, but no point letting them go dry, not with a well alongside the cabin. Mary filled the bucket and held it up for Peter, then Paul, rubbing their muzzles and running her free hand over their strong necks. Muttering words that didn't mean anything as they lapped up the water. She'd lost sight of Amelia. No matter. No harm letting the woman poke around. Get to know the cow and calf, and the homestead. It would all be her responsibility soon enough.

Behind her, a screen door swung shut and boot heels drummed across the front porch. Amelia, coming out of the cabin.

"He told me he'd ordered a new stove," she called. "It's already here and it's beautiful. The place is short on furniture, but we can—"

She was interrupted by the bark of a dog. That darned Jess, on the trail of something.

A rooster crowed. Both women followed the sound. To the east a couple of hundred yards stood a hedge of lilacs and honeysuckle, beginning to leaf out. Mary squinted, and through a gap in the hedge made out a whitewashed house, a sight nicer than this cabin. A woman shouted and a hen flew above the shrubbery, then disappeared from view.

The woman came barreling through the gap, pregnant belly bulging her blue calico. "Go on, you nasty old thing," she yelled, flapping her arms. Her dark apron fluttered with the movement. "You're not getting one more of my hens or another egg—"

She stopped, her words and hands frozen in midair. In the distance, children's voices rose and fell.

"Oh, goodness. Good Lord, me," she said at the sight of

Mary. "Didn't hear the wagon. Thought it was that fox come back to finish the dinner he started."

Then she spotted Amelia standing on the porch. Her cheeks, pink from exertion, now burned dark red and her eyes narrowed in her thin face. "So it's true, then. The thieving interloper has got himself a bride. Well, I'll tell you, missy, you may stand there looking all sweet and innocent in that blue suit, but you're as guilty as he is for taking what belongs to us. To Johannes and my Henrik. To my family." She slapped her open palm against her breast.

"Mrs. Bergen," Mary began, but Mrs. Henrik Bergen was in no mood to be interrupted.

"Don't you start with me, Mary. I know there's talk and I know you've heard it. But we won't stand for it."

For talk? Good luck with that. Or did she mean something else?

At that moment, Jess came racing around the side of the cabin, a cluster of feathers and feet hanging from his mouth.

What had the fool dog done? He ran to Mary and dropped the wet, mangled hen at her feet.

Mrs. Bergen let out a cry. Mary didn't dare look at her. She picked up the lifeless hen. Held it out.

"I'll make it up to you, first chance I get," she said.

The woman snatched the dead bird from Mary's hands.

"You will," she said, glowering first at Mary and then at Amelia Morgan, standing on the front porch of her future home. "Both of you."

• • •

"You sure you don't want a swig?" Mary held out the brown clay jug. They'd stopped at the top of the drive, out of Mrs. Henrik Bergen's sight. "Settles the nerves."

Amelia started to shake her head, then grabbed the jug

and took a swallow. Not a big glug, like it was water, but not a mincing sip. Girl didn't even cough. Just handed the jug back and wiped her mouth with the back of her hand.

"Thank you."

Mary corked the whiskey and tucked the jug under the seat. She turned the team onto the road. A small hawk swooped in front of them but the horses didn't flinch.

"What do you know that you're not telling me?" Amelia asked, her voice low but steady. "About the Bergens, and George. And that horrid woman."

Ever since Mrs. Bergen had stalked back through the hedge, muttering in a mix of English and what Mary assumed was Norwegian, though she'd detected no accent in the woman's English, she'd been rooting around in her mind for stray rumors and gossip. Plenty of people who looked right past her didn't hesitate to talk near her, as if she didn't have ears. More like they didn't have eyes, not quite seeing her. Even some of the nuns were that way.

"Not much I can tell you," she began.

"Can't or won't?"

The younger woman's challenge surprised her. "Can't tell you what I don't know. I lived at the Mission for close to ten years, doing laundry and the garden and other jobs. Hauled freight. Even did some hunting and trapping when I first got out here, when food was scarce. Got acquainted with a lot of folks. Even the ones who aren't Catholic, or who hate the Catholics, occasionally have business with the Jesuits or the sisters. And now I deliver the mail."

"So you knew about the correspondence between George and me?"

"Child, I deliver the mail. I don't read it. Besides, he's new down here. You said it yourself."

"True. He arrived less than two months ago."

Between them on the wagon seat, Jess let out a soft groan. Dreaming of the chicken that had been taken away from him.

"You called her Mrs. Bergen," Amelia continued. "The wife?"

"Sister-in-law. Henrik and Johannes are brothers who filed on adjoining claims. Joe wasn't married, far as I know. I do know"—she shifted the reins from one hand to the other—"that Joe selling out and moving on has set a few tongues wagging, but no one seems to know the truth of what happened."

Amelia made a pondering sound. "I only caught a glimpse of the other house, but it looked bigger. Painted. Why paint the one and not the other? Though I imagine winter is as hard on paint as sun is."

"And the wind," Mary said. All these years, it still tore through her.

"Was there a rift, then, between the brothers? Why would Joe sell to George, rather than to Henrik?"

That was the question. And, she suspected, the burr under Mrs. Henrik's saddle.

"I never heard," Mary said, and it was true.

"So where is this Joe now?"

But Mary had no answer for that, either. She shook her head and changed the subject.

"Tell me about them books you brought."

"A few of my favorites, for the train, and for the winter ahead. Jane Austen. Dickens and Twain. I could only bring a few, but George said not to worry. There are books in Montana." She smiled, clearly clinging fondly to a reassuring comment. "My old teacher gave me the newest by Henry James, and a book of poetry. How much farther to the Mission?"

"Not long now. Will Mr. Reynolds be meeting you there?"

"Tomorrow. I believe he's gone to look at some cattle. He hopes to raise a herd—a small one at first, with more to come."

"You got a date for this wedding?"

"As soon as possible," Amelia said, and nothing more.

The last of the Jesuits' cattle grazed on a broad, gently sloping hillside. Mary pointed out Birdtail Rock, its distinctive shape a sign that they were nearly at their destination.

Then the Mission came into view. The sisters had worked miracles. Not to take anything away from the Jesuits, who'd established the Mission nearly forty years ago to serve the Blackfeet. They'd been forced to move several times, as the result of tensions and broken promises and she didn't know what else. Even this spot, its fourth, had gotten off to a troubled start. The Jesuits had built the chapel and the log cabins, later giving them over for the original girls' school. But the sisters had turned the vision into bricks on the ground and books in the classroom. Music on the air and the stage of the small opera house. They'd built the laundry and kitchen, and tamed the place.

Amadeus had worked herself ragged begging for money, especially in those early years, and she had succeeded. Mount Angela, the grand three-story stone building that held the convent, classrooms, and sleeping rooms for the boarders and guests, pure took Mary's breath away. Amadeus was particularly proud of the fancy roofline—mansard, she called it—and the tower at the main entrance, topped with a cross-crowned dome that one of the young Italian Jesuits said reminded him of the churches of Rome. Mary was partial to the arched windows that overlooked the grasslands and hillsides, and the wide steps where a body could sit and drink it all in.

All of it fine as any school in the state, she was sure, the equal of the buildings back at the Motherhouse.

And a sight better than the Jesuits' square wooden dormitory and blocky stone school, if you asked her.

"Oh, my," was all Amelia said, and that was enough.

Mary pulled the wagon up to the towering stone building. A young nun emerged, a broad smile on her face, barely visible for the swath of starched white fabric that circled her face and covered her neck.

"Mary! So good to see you! And you've brought us something far more important than the mail. You've brought us a visitor." She opened her arms, the wide black outer sleeves of her habit spreading like a crow's wings as she gestured to their surroundings, as unexpected a contrast to the sweeping prairies and rugged bluffs and buttes as even Amelia's beloved authors could have imagined. "Welcome to St. Peter's. I'm Sister Louisine. What a beautiful day for your arrival. Come. Let's get you settled."

Amelia shot Mary an amused glance. No introductions needed when Louisine was around.

"Wait a moment, Mary," Amelia said, reaching over the side of the wagon and opening her carpetbag. She pulled out a flour sack and carefully unwrapped the contents. Handed Mary a small blue jar. "Crab apple jelly, from the farm. I put it up myself, last fall. A token of my thanks."

"You're mighty welcome. You take care now, you and that rose. Hate to see it wither, after such a long trip."

When the boys Louisine had summoned finished unloading the wagon, laughing and shouting as they staggered under the weight of Amelia's trunk, Mary took the team to the barn. Unhitched the horses and gave their muzzles a good rub before turning them over to another mess of boys for food and water and a good rubdown. Tucked the jelly jar safely into the box beneath the seat, next to her jug, and grabbed the mailbag. She had work to do.

• • •

Even better than sleeping in her old log cabin again was waking up Sunday morning and knowing she had no route to drive, no schedule to keep. Nobody was counting on her for a thing. Mary stretched her arms out and arched her back. No one expected her to feed the chickens or gather eggs, to chop wood for the cookstove or milk the cow. They didn't even expect her to attend Mass, though if Mother Amadeus were here, she'd go. But the Mother Superior had gone to visit another mission, checking on the sisters and their progress.

It would do her no harm to stop in the church for a minute or two. Remind God she was alive and kicking.

But first things first. Mary made her way across the compound, returning greetings from those about the place—a young nun on an errand, a priest striding quickly across the field, a pair of older girls in matching dresses that ended an inch or two below the knee giggling as they made their way to the cookhouse with their basket full of eggs. It was a wonder, what Amadeus and the others had accomplished here on this strange, empty land.

In the corral, Peter and Paul mingled with the Mission's horses. Soon, the place would buzz with activity, the corral full. Though parents of the Indian children who attended the boarding school didn't visit often—the reservation was a good distance—the settlers treated it as their gathering place, coming for Mass and staying for Sunday dinner and gossip.

The big gray ambled over to the fence to greet her, the chestnut not far behind. She pulled an apple and her knife out of her pocket and split it in two. Cradled a half in each hand and held them out.

"Don't let the others know you're special," she said as the horses gobbled up the fruit. She lingered a long moment, rubbing her hands over their ears and down their necks.

Though the sisters now used the chapel in Mount Angela, Mary preferred the simplicity of the original church, barely a stone's throw from the corral. Its white exterior, a mix of clapboard and hewn logs, and plain wood interior felt holy and familiar. She'd sneak in there.

"Good morning, Mary," a voice called, and she turned to see Louisine sitting beneath a tree a few feet away, a prayer book in her lap. On a nearby bench, Amelia sat with a man. George Reynolds. She wore the blue suit again, no doubt brushed within an inch of its life to clean off the traveling dust. No hat today, her dark hair neatly rolled and put up. Reynolds was slender and long-legged—he'd tower over his bride-to-be—and his dark hair and mustache were neatly trimmed. He inclined his head toward Amelia as he spoke, and she laughed with what sounded like real pleasure.

"Can't let them spend time together without a chaperone, can we, even with the angels watching from the bell tower?" A lilt in Louisine's voice gave away the tease. Mary grunted. The sound traveled and the young couple turned their heads.

"Mary," Amelia said, rising. "Good to see you this morning. May I introduce my fiancé, Mr. George Reynolds?"

"Mary," he said, standing beside Amelia. Handsome enough, Mary decided, to attract a woman but not enough to make females swoon or men jealous and distrustful. He nodded, though he did not extend a hand. "I don't believe I've had the pleasure, although your reputation precedes you."

That could mean a lot of things. His tone did not betray whether he'd heard the good, or the not so good.

"I was telling George about our encounter with Mrs. Bergen," Amelia said.

"I should have warned you," George said. "But I never imagined you'd stop."

"Oh, Mary wouldn't have. She has a better sense of propriety than I do, but I quite insisted, didn't I?"

"That you did," Mary replied.

Reynolds took Amelia's hand. "You've been here far longer than I have, Mary, so I'm sure it's no surprise to you that Mrs. Bergen resents me. She would resent anyone taking over her brother-in-law's homestead, no matter what the circumstances."

A prickle rose on the back of Mary's neck. *Circumstances* was like *reputation*. It could mean a lot of things.

"As I was telling Amelia," he said, "I've just returned from a trip up past Choteau to see a man about buying some cattle. Time to build my herd."

Show-toe. Northwest of here, closer to the mountains and the Blackfeet Reservation. Mary had not been there.

"We're going to be ranchers," Amelia said. "And farmers. At least I know I can be useful with the garden and the milking."

She freed her hand from Reynolds's grasp and slipped her arm through his, and the couple exchanged a warm look. Mrs. Henrik Bergen might think him a thieving interloper, but he seemed right enough, although many a cruel heart hid behind a pleasant face. Mary hoped this business with the Bergens didn't become too difficult. Jess's taste for chicken hadn't helped. She'd see if she could find a healthy young hen to offer in apology.

The settlers began to arrive, filling the air with the clip of horses' hooves and the rattle and roll of wagon wheels. Greetings were exchanged. Boys took charge of horses, girls took baskets of food from the women. For a few hours, the Mission would become a bustling little settlement tucked between the wide prairie and the wider sky, ringed by the flat-topped buttes and the high, jagged rocks.

Mary had lost her chance for a private word with God. Had she her druthers, she'd have slipped away and gone down to Birch Creek to visit with Him. Him and the red-winged blackbirds, her old friends from Tennessee. But Amelia had stretched out a hand to draw her in, and Mary had not the steel to refuse the gesture. She and Louisine followed the couple to Mount Angela and into the chapel.

Always took her by surprise, seeing the shroud of angels and other figures draped in blue and gold surrounding the tabernacle. Statues of angels and saints stood atop wooden columns, and dark, grim paintings of the Stations of the Cross hung on the walls. Wooden kneelers. No pews.

The air inside already hot and sticky with the breath of the Sunday crowd, Mary knelt and rose, muttered the prayers, sang the hymns. She hadn't heard a word of fancy Latin or seen a beaded rosary before taking the job with Amadeus's brother, Judge Dunne, and his pretty wife. After Mrs. Dunne's death, she'd taken the children to Amadeus at the Motherhouse in Toledo, where the sisters' rhythms had governed her days, but she figured this was the same God she'd met in the cotton fields and Sunday meetings in the tobacco sheds, even if the trappings were different.

She stood in back, as always. From here, she could watch and ponder free of others' gazes. It hadn't been a full day since she'd picked Amelia up and driven her out to lodge with the sisters. That gave Mary a sense of responsibility, although her duty had been discharged once the girl was safely delivered. Young woman, though she seemed like a girl to Mary, and not just because Mary was an old woman. Sixty-five, more or less. Weren't no one at the Mission even close to being as old as she was.

Besides, Mary liked the girl. And she understood how it was to leave a place where there was no room for you.

Mary spotted Louisine kneeling beside the other sisters. She'd felt the same kind of protectiveness over her when they first met, at the Motherhouse. Still felt it toward young Josie, one of the first pupils at the school, now graduated and teaching on the reservation.

And to Amadeus, now past fifty. Good Lord. Had it really been close to thirty years since they'd met? Amadeus had already left her brother's house and taken vows when Mary went to work for the family, though of course she and the young nun had seen each other often. Funny. She didn't feel the closeness to the judge's own daughters that she felt for Amadeus and her flock.

When the final prayers ended, Mary slipped out and made for the creek. Jess had been waiting and bounded ahead to the well-trod path, knowing where they were going almost before she did. Near the water's edge, by a clump of golden willow, she tucked up her skirt. Pulled off her boots and the thick wool socks that kept the boots from rubbing her corns and bones. Shame some of the padding she carried elsewhere couldn't be on her feet, where she needed it. The big rock waited where it ought to be and she settled her backside onto the rough perch, then plunged her feet into the cold water, the shock rippling through her, though not unpleasantly.

Jess splashed and shook his tail, and wet droplets hit her face.

"Off with you, dog," she muttered, but in truth, she loved Birch Creek as much as he did. Since moving into town a few years back, she'd found a few spots where she could work her way down to the river and wade in. They called the

Missouri the Big Muddy for a reason, and she relished the lap of the water at her calves and the thick mud oozing between her toes. But these cool, clear waters were like medicine. Balm for the sin-sick soul, in the words of the hymn.

Mary soaked her feet for a while, then found a patch of shade by a cluster of sarvisberry and chokecherry bushes and laid down to rest her eyes. When she woke, it was to the sight of a splint basket and a swath of black fabric.

"I expected I'd find you down here," Louisine said, "though you hid yourself well."

Mary sat up. "Good thing you kept your eyes on that basket," she said, nodding toward Jess, bright-eyed at the prospect of food.

"Oh, I know him better than that," Louisine said. She spread a small checkered cloth on the ground, then lifted a covered dish out of the basket. "I brought you some of everything, plus a couple of meat pies for later. And apple cake from Mrs. Whitney at the mill. She particularly wanted you to have a piece."

"And I particularly want it," Mary said. "This evening, with a spot of cream and a spot of whiskey."

Louisine had eaten with the nuns and the other women, so she chatted while Mary ate. She told who was there, who'd brought what food, and who'd been sick or traveling or had some story to tell—all the things women talked about when they got together. Mary desperately wanted to know how they responded to Amelia Morgan, what they said about George Reynolds, and their opinion of Mrs. Henrik and her brother-in-law, but no point asking. Louisine would get to it in her own time.

Finally, the young nun turned to what she knew Mary would most want to hear.

"I have to say, Miss Morgan fit in nicely. Women with

sisters often do, don't you think?" Louisine herself was the youngest of four, raised with other female relatives in the house. Mary figured she'd never been allowed to get a word in edgewise. Add in the hours spent in silent prayer, and no wonder she chattered on. She had a lot of lost talking time to make up for.

"She helped the women set out their dishes and carry in what the sisters made, and was as complimentary as she could be." Louisine didn't bother waiting for Mary to reply. "The women were very interested in her clothing—her suit isn't fancy, but it's newer and more fashionable than anything they have. Though they were surprised to hear that she brought no wedding quilt. She's got a top, partially pieced. Mrs. Whitney at the mill is going to speak to her sister-in-law, Mrs. Whitney from the general store, about finishing it."

"That's mighty nice," Mary said, her mouth around a ham bun. The general store sold fabric and thread, of course, and that particular Mrs. Whitney was an expert quilter and seamstress. Curious, though, that Amelia had been sent off to marry without a finished quilt.

"Courtship by correspondence. Or almost—that's how it began, but they did meet face-to-face last fall. Turns out that's how Mrs. Carlton met her husband, and Sister Thomas Joseph said her widowed father met his new wife that way."

Mary slipped Jess a bite of ham.

"Mr. Reynolds being new in the valley," Louisine went on, "they didn't have a lot to say about him. He has a brother working up somewhere north, but no one here has met him."

"Benjamin," Mary said.

"Yes, that's it. Miss Morgan asked about the Bergens, being the closest neighbors and all. It was Johannes Bergen who sold his stake to George Reynolds. Mrs. Carlton said that Johannes—they call him Joe—hasn't been seen for weeks, since well before the last snowstorm. Took his money and left, I imagine. It will be nice for Miss Morgan to have another woman so close."

So Amelia had not mentioned their run-in with Mrs. Henrik. Too soon for word to have spread, but it would.

"I wouldn't know," Mary said, though Henrik Bergen's missus had made her feelings clear. She reached for a meat pie, then stopped herself. Best to keep it for later. Mary was a good cook. Her restaurant hadn't failed because of the food. It failed because she hadn't had the heart to charge what she ought, or even to charge at all if she thought the customer couldn't pay. The barkeeper had flat out told her people were cheating her. Mr. Whitney at the general store had said it was hard to know sometimes who was genuinely in need and who was taking advantage of generosity, but if she wanted to stay in business, she had to have a harder heart. Maybe so, but if it was a choice between feeding people and begrudging them, well, that was a choice she wasn't interested in making.

But it sure was nice when someone else saved her the trouble of doing all the work for just herself.

"I'd best be setting off," she said and reached for her boots. "Need to stop by the chicken coop on the way."

Louisine carried the basket, the meat pies and cake safely tucked inside. The dog ran ahead. He knew better than to eat the sisters' hens. What had gotten into him yesterday, Mary had no idea.

Had Mrs. Henrik's harsh words about George Reynolds been set off by the deeds of the dog, or was there some truth to her accusations?

Speaking of George Reynolds. There he was, crossing the field with Amelia.

The dog had caught up with a group of boys, barking at their heels as they threw a ball. The ball rolled between one boy's legs and he chased after it, running directly in front of Reynolds. The boy tripped, tumbling haplessly. Reynolds steered Amelia out of the way and leaped over the boy. Amelia clapped her hands to her mouth, then when it was apparent that her fiancé was unharmed, she turned to speak to the boy, sitting on the ground, the ball in one hand.

"Well, he's light on his feet, Mr. Reynolds is," Louisine said. "I wonder if Miss Morgan likes to dance."

An older nun charged toward the boy, clearly intent on a reprimand.

"No, no," George Reynolds said, holding out a hand. "Let boys be boys, especially on a Sunday."

"A day for prayer," the nun said.

"And for play," Amelia interjected.

The boy took the standoff as an opportunity to escape and ran back to his friends, who greeted him with shouts and playful jeers. The nun nodded stiffly to the couple and marched off, disapproval in the sway of her long black skirt.

"I'll make sure he isn't punished," Louisine said.

On the way to the coop, Mary described the encounter with Mrs. Henrik and why she needed a hen.

"Oh, my," Louisine said. "Yes, that's only fair. You might get the opportunity to ask her why Johannes sold his place and what she thinks Mr. Reynolds has done. Or at the least, to find out what kind of neighbor she'll be."

But of that, Mary was sure. The difficult kind.

They found a young hen, and Mary stuffed the bird into her basket, hoping it would not be missed until morning, when no one would think to blame her or Jess. And much as Louisine loved to talk, she was not a tattler. Mary thanked the young nun for the food and conversation and said her goodbyes, then headed to her old cabin. Collected the jug and jelly jar, which fit nicely in the basket. At the corral, she tucked her things under the wagon seat and began to hitch up the team.

"Mary," Amelia called, hurrying toward her. "I'm glad to catch you. George has gone to talk to one of the priests about the marriage ceremony. I—I have a favor to ask."

"I'm listening, child," Mary said.

"I don't mind admitting I'm still shaken by Mrs. Bergen's comments. They were awfully harsh, and I do wonder what she meant. No one said anything unkind about George today—"

"They wouldn't now, would they? Not in front of you."

"No, of course not. But I did wonder . . ." Her words trailed off. "Is there a chance Mrs. Bergen is wrong? That she was talking about someone else, maybe his brother? I don't know much about him. No one seems to."

If she knew nothing about Benjamin Reynolds, why think the harsh accusations had been intended for him? And why would Mrs. Bergen criticize a man who by all accounts had not yet visited the area?

Was Amelia grasping for a way to keep on believing the best about the man she was about to marry? Did she have her own doubts, doubts she was looking to excuse?

Surely not. Surely she would not have come all this way without being sure of her own mind.

But before Mary could say anything, a male voice called her name. "Mary! Let me give you a hand."

The two women turned to see a man of about twenty-five trotting toward them, a shock of brown hair flopping on his forehead.

"Thomas," Mary said. "You're a sight for sore eyes. And right in time to hitch these ornery old cusses for me. Have you met Miss Morgan?"

Thomas grinned at Mary, then introduced himself to the newcomer. "Thomas Whitney, Miss Morgan. You are as pretty as your picture. Welcome to Montana."

Amelia held out her hand, a soft blush rising in her cheeks. "Thank you, Mr. Whitney. I suppose word of new arrivals travels quickly."

"Ain't none of us traveling anywhere, slow or fast, if these horses don't get hitched," Mary said. "What are you doing here of a Sunday?"

"Now that George is back, I've been helping him make that cabin of his into a house. He showed me Miss Morgan's picture, pleased as he could be." Thomas got to work. "I came out here today to see my folks, when they drove over for Sunday Mass. I've been building things since I was knee-high to a wagon wheel." He aimed this last at Amelia, as Mary knew well his love of tinkering.

She'd been new in the territory—and it had still been a territory then—when she first met Thomas and his younger brother, the mill owner's sons. Her first summer in Montana. He'd been shy of her and her blackness then, but once the boys started at the mission school, he'd gotten over that. Before classes or after the noon meal, when other boys had been playing games or running down to the creek, Thomas had pestered the men working on whatever building was going up at the time to let him do small tasks for them, and he'd learned by watching. When he left school, he'd hired on to help build the new hotel in Cascade, staying with his uncle and aunt above the general store. Since then, he'd built just about anything anyone needed, including working at the other missions, at Amadeus's request. George Reynolds had chosen wisely.

And Thomas had always been quick to give her a hand.

"There. All set." The wagon hitched, Thomas pulled two small, wrinkled apples out of his pocket, one for each horse. Gave the dog's ear a quick tug. "Sorry, Jess. I've got nothing for you."

"He's had his share today," Mary said. She gave the dog a boost into the wagon and climbed up beside him. He smelled of wet mud. She plucked a small stick out of his chest fur and flicked it away.

"Mary," Amelia said, drawing close and lowering her voice. "Do let me know what you hear."

"Don't you listen to gossip. Listen to your heart." She picked up the reins and called to her team. "On with you now." When they reached the road, scarcely needing her to guide them, Mary stole a glance over her shoulder. Back at the corral, Thomas and Amelia waved.

And Mary couldn't help but think the winds of change blew fickle sometimes.

• • •

"If that girl can travel for days to a part of the country she ain't never seen to marry a man she met once, you can face a biddy and give her a chicken to make up for the one your fool dog stole," Mary told herself as she steered the wagon over the ridge and veered right where the trail split. The chicken—a young hen—was safely wrapped in cloth in the basket tucked beneath her skirt, out of Jess's reach.

The differences between the Henrik Bergen house and Joe's weathered cabin—now George's—went far beyond paint. The difference between a married man and a bachelor. Two-story, frame, its white paint unchipped, a gingerbread scroll in the peaked roof and another on the screen door. A rocker on the porch, a lace curtain in the window. Two small apple trees, staked against the wind, in front. This house looked like it belonged in town.

Ahead of her, too intent to hear the wagon, a young boy

rolled a wooden hoop with a stick. The hoop came nearly to his chest. It rolled down the hardpack, then hit a stone and bounced away, tottered, and fell on its side. Only then did he notice her.

"Pa!" he shouted. "Pa!"

The screen door opened and a man emerged, pulling his suspenders up onto his broad shoulders.

"Hush, son. Your mother is resting," Henrik Bergen said. A girl in a blue dress, three or four years old, stood behind him in the doorway, her thumb in her mouth. Barefoot, like the boy. "Delivering the mail on a Sunday, Mary?"

Had his wife not told him of yesterday's encounter, or explained the missing hen?

"That's the dog that ate Ma's hen," the boy shouted before Mary could reply. "The other woman was with her, the one who's going to marry the man who took—"

"Be still," Henrik said and the boy froze, mouth open. The stick dangled in his small hand, the hoop forgotten in the grass. Henrik waited for Mary to speak, his blue eyes intent on her, his broad, wind-chapped face impassive.

"The boy's right, Mr. Bergen," she said, hating the croak in her voice that made her sound uncertain. "Yesterday I delivered Miss Amelia Morgan to the Mission to stay for a spell, before she marries Mr. George Reynolds. On the way, we stopped for a gander, and my dog helped himself to a hen. I've brought one to replace it."

A shadow crossed the big man's face, though whether at the news of the purloined poultry, thoughts of his brother and the homestead he'd sold, or the name George Reynolds, Mary could not guess.

She lifted the chicken out of the basket. No longer confined, it raised a wing, freeing itself from the cloth, and let out a squawk. Mary held it toward the boy, who dropped his stick and reached up for it. A moment later, the hen was running around on the ground, cackling and flapping at the freedom.

Beside her on the wagon seat, Jess stirred. "Stay," Mary barked, and bless the dog, he stayed.

"Well," Henrik said, his mouth and jaw tight. "That's thoughtful of you."

His accent gave him away as an immigrant. Mary had only seen him a handful of times, his brother not much more, and could not remember hearing either man speak.

"Is your brother staying with you now that he's sold his place?" she asked.

"Sold." Henrik spat out the word.

"Should I go get—" the boy began, but his father cut the air quickly with one hand and the boy fell silent again.

"He is gone mining," Henrik said. "In California."

One theory Mary had heard. "I wish him luck."

Henrik made a noise that told her what he thought of that. She gathered her reins.

"Please tell your missus I'm sorry for the trouble my dog caused. I've done my best to make it right. This hen here come from the sisters' flock and I tended 'em for years, so I can promise you they know how to lay a good egg. And I hope all goes well with her when her time comes."

Might be nice to have a woman living next door then. But no point saying so.

"Here we go now," she called to the team.

"Mary." Henrik raised a hand to stop her. "I wish the girl well. None of this is her fault. And I thank you for your kindness."

By "the girl," he had to mean Amelia. But what did he mean by "none of this"? None of what?

Mary nodded. As the horses swung wide to make the

turn, she spotted a cabin behind the house. Almost a twin to the one on George Reynolds's place. The original homestead cabin, required by law. Henrik had replaced his; Joe had not, though it was big enough to give Reynolds a good start on a real house.

Henrik said Joe was gone mining. But unless she was sore mistaken, the boy had been about to go get someone. Not his resting mother, she was sure. Uncle Joe?

If Joe Bergen was still around, there would be talk. It hadn't yet reached her ears, but she could take care of that, if she listened in the right places.

No, she told herself. She'd made right what she could. Now it was time to keep her nose out of other people's business.

• • •

A few days later, after she'd finished her route, Mary delivered the outgoing mail to the stable for the stage driver to collect. She saw to her team and wagon, then stepped into the street. A gust whipped her skirt and she snatched it back.

She narrowed her eyes against the onslaught of fine dust and dirt and scanned the sky. Not a cloud anywhere. With nothing in the way to slow it down, the wind just kept blowing. She held on to her hat and stepped onto the boardwalk, Jess trotting beside her.

How would Amelia Morgan fare in these winds, Amelia and that rose?

Mary trudged up to the general store, which was also the post office and the Whitney family home. The dog lay down outside the door without being told. He was so smart he scared her sometimes. Unlike some people.

Inside, Mr. Whitney—uncle to Thomas, brother to the mill owner—stood behind the counter, in his usual white shirt and brocade vest. She'd done a fair bit of laundry in her life and had to admire Mrs. Whitney's ability to keep the man's shirts so clean, considering all the boxes and crates he lifted and hauled in a day, the grime and sawdust he rubbed up against. The smells of newsprint and molasses mingled in the air.

A pair of women's voices drifted toward her. Mrs. Whitney's gentle tone she knew well, but the other she couldn't identify. Mary squeezed around a display of canned goods to where she could see without being seen.

"I do hope you'll come," Mrs. Whitney was saying. "I'll help her add a border to finish the top, then we'll set up the frame and stitch a nice pattern."

Must be the wedding quilt Louisine had mentioned.

"We'll have a luncheon and a good chat," she went on. "And I have an idea there might be a baby quilt in the making as well."

A soft scuffling caught Mary's attention. She looked down to see a little girl with wispy blond hair staring at her, a peppermint stick in one chubby hand.

Mary held a finger to her lips. The child nodded and stuck the candy in her mouth. Now she knew who the woman was. Mrs. Henrik Bergen.

Mrs. Bergen's reply was clear. "And is this wedding quilt for that interloper and the woman who's come all the way out here from God knows where to snatch prosperity from the hands of those who worked for it? Have you seen how he's gussying up a perfectly fine cabin for her, with a new stove and factory-made furniture? She must think pretty highly of herself. Next thing you know, she'll be wanting an icebox in the house."

Mary had been right. The quilt was meant for George Reynolds and Amelia Morgan.

"What do we know about her, anyway?" Mrs. Bergen continued. "Is she in on all this?"

In on what? It was almost the same phrase her husband had used, signifying a shared grievance. And what was this nonsense about Amelia's pride? Mary had believed Amelia's story of the family's hard life back East, of being one too many daughters and not seeing a future for herself amid the struggle. She'd seen the astonishment on the young woman's face at the size of the cabin addition and heard her exclaim over the new stove. It was hardly extravagant—even with the addition, the house would be smaller than Henrik's. Cascade boasted several larger homes. They were all dolls' houses compared to the grand homes Mary had seen in Ohio.

A case of the talk saying more about the speaker than the one spoken of? Maybe so. Amelia had appeared as honest and upright as you'd want a young woman to be. Mary had spied no hint of avarice or greed, nothing boastful in her words or demeanor.

But something had riled Mrs. Bergen, and her husband, too.

Mary was turning the question over in her mind when she realized the child had disappeared. Saw her now, tugging at her mother's skirt and pointing.

Both women looked her way.

"Hello, Mary," Mrs. Whitney said. No surprise she was the first to speak. A pretty woman with sad eyes, generous in the way women who'd wanted children but been disappointed often were. She'd always welcomed Mary, and not just because Mary drove the postal route and frequently made deliveries for the store.

"Mary," Mrs. Bergen said, her voice as full of starch as Mr. Whitney's collar. "I suppose I owe you thanks for the hen you brought by. It took to its new henhouse nicely, and gave us an egg this morning. More to come, I hope."

"Yes, ma'am," Mary said. "Came from the sisters' flock. They got good chickens."

Mrs. Bergen turned back to the shopkeeper's wife. "I thank you for taking the milk and butter on trade. My husband will pick up our order later." She took the child by the hand and nearly dragged her to the door, the child looking back at Mary with serious eyes. What was she thinking? You never could tell.

"Careful of the wind," Mary called. "It's blowin' awful."

"Well," Mrs. Whitney said after the door had closed behind the Bergens. "I do hope we can all excuse her. You know how some women get when they're that far along."

"That's your kind heart speaking, my dear," her husband said, and she gave him an affectionate smile.

"They're none too pleased to have new neighbors," Mary ventured, "but it ain't George Reynolds's fault that he came along right when Joe Bergen decided to sell, is it?"

"I suspect Henrik and his wife think otherwise," Whitney said. "Homesteading was his plan, and he's made a fair go of it. But his brother . . ." The words trailed off.

"I hear Joe's gone after a mining claim," Mary said.

"Many a man's chased that dream and come back poorer for it," Whitney replied.

Joe Bergen had proved up. He could come and go without losing anything more than a planting season. If he'd wanted to sell, why not sell to his brother? Mrs. Henrik had made clear, standing in front of Joe's cabin, that she thought her husband had a stake in the place.

"Brothers can be mighty different," Mary said. "Henrik and Joe get along?"

"Far as I know," Whitney said. "But some men aren't made to stay put."

True enough. There were doers and dreamers in this world, and men who went whichever way the wind blew. Women, too, though women didn't have so many choices. Couldn't just up and go, unless they had the money to support themselves.

The talk of brothers reminded Mary of a question nagging at her. "Mr. Reynolds has a brother, don't he? Somewhere up north. You hear anything of him?"

"Not a word." Whitney polished the gleaming counter with one of his wife's snow white cloths. "Nobody here knew a peep about George when he came in, said he'd taken over Joe's place. Late March, first of April. Made a nice order of supplies. A few weeks back, he said he had a future bride on the way and ordered a new cookstove and some furniture. Stove came in on the freight train from Helena a week or so ago. Just in time, he said, and I guess he was right." The shopkeeper gave his wife the smile of a contentedly married man.

The door opened and a woman entered. She nodded at Mary and handed Mrs. Whitney a list. Mary took a can of peaches from the display and held it up for Whitney to see and add to her account. You primed the pump, you'd better pay for whatever trickled out.

Outside, the wind had not died down. It rippled Jess's ears as they rounded the corner and headed for the Silver Dollar.

"Mary, you dry already?" the saloonkeeper called when she entered. Then he spotted the peaches in her hand. "Where's your jug?"

"Next to my chair by the stove. Thought it might be nice to sit at the bar for a change. Listen to your blather."

He rolled his eyes and reached for a bottle. Filled a glass with amber liquid and slid it in front of her. Light and shadows glinted in the mirror behind him and off his bald head. Since moving into town, Mary hadn't had much occasion to drink in the saloon. But it was a good place to hear folks talk. Men folks. People spoke disapprovingly of women's talk, but to Mary's ear, men were the bigger gossips. Though maybe their words weren't quite so harsh.

A handful of men sat around one of the oak tables, a bottle and glasses in front of them. A fellow from out Lepley Creek, who gave her a nod, and a trio of ranchers from across the river. And as she had anticipated, Henrik Bergen, sitting alone in the corner, looking redder in the face than he had on Sunday. His glass was nearly empty.

The saloon was small and her hearing was sharp, but even so, she angled her bulk to better catch the sense of things.

"Lucked out this past winter, we did," one of the ranchers from across the river said. "Lost one cow. Got herself caught in a gully and busted a leg. It's a shame—she still had a few more years of calving in her—but it could have been worse."

Mary took a small sip and welcomed the heat that slid down her gullet. The wind had a bite that made the spring day feel like December. If these men were going to natter on about the weather, she was going to have to drink real slow.

"Lucky you don't run your herd up by Buffalo Falls," another rancher said. "Fellow up there lost half a dozen head. Got trapped by the old pishkin and drifted right over the falls." He made a diving gesture with one chapped hand.

"Open range is closed, boys," the first rancher said. "Ain't no use pretending otherwise."

They griped about the loss of a way of life most of them had never known, their talk drifting this way and that, cutting in and over each other.

"Saw that brother of yours riding down by Black Butte a

few days ago," the man from Lepley Creek called to Henrik. "Thought you said he'd gone to California."

"That's daft," the first rancher said. "I took the wife to Great Falls a week ago to catch the train. Her mother's ailing and she's going back to help out. I spotted Joe in the alley behind a saloon on Central Avenue, none too steady on his feet."

Statehood had brought an end to legal gambling, but there were back doors. Men would find a way.

The room hushed.

"Didn't think he had anything left to lose," the man continued.

The silence took on an edge. Mary watched the reflections in the mirror—the way the other men held their tongues, faces still but for their eyes, darting between the rancher and Henrik Bergen.

After a long moment, Henrik pushed back his chair, its legs scraping the rough lumber of the saloon floor. He crossed to the other table and the bartender slid toward the end of the bar, ready to step around and step in.

But Henrik Bergen didn't raise his fist to the man. Instead, he reached for the bottle, raised it to his lips and drained it, then slammed it back down. Pulled a coin from his pocket and tossed it on the table, where it spun like a top before finally falling on its side, an echo of the hoop Mary had seen his son playing with only a few days ago.

By the time the silver stopped spinning, he was gone.

• • •

Mary left the can of peaches at the bar. The saloonkeeper was clear that he didn't trade for whiskey or give credit. Cold hard cash, by golly. But for her, he sometimes bent his own rules.

She and Jess worked their way down to the river. Thoughts flowed better alongside water, or so she told herself. The dog loved to run up and down the banks, chasing the pelicans and the other birds, all floating out of his reach and perfectly safe from him. Unlike that poor chicken.

She sat on the riverbank and pulled out her pipe. Filled the bowl. Lit it and drew. Funny how the first puff took her back. Seemed like smells worked that way—you caught a whiff of something, good or bad, and before you knew it, your mind had gone off on its own to somewhere else. How on earth you'd got there you didn't know, until a word or two filtered through the fog of your memory. The smell of newly turned dirt always minded her of the fields when she'd been a child. Then other smells from the past would come rushing in. The hot reek of laundry day. The musky odor of the old lady's room in the first household where she'd worked after the war, that no amount of airing could clear out. The muck of the river on the steamship where she'd been a chambermaid. The *Robert E. Lee*. Name still made her snicker. It was the captain who'd introduced her to Judge Dunne, and who'd smoked good, rich tobacco, nothing like the half-green stuff the men had smoked in her girlhood.

This tobacco, this smoke. This river. It was all hers.

Down on the water, a pelican squawked at Jess and he barked in return.

She took another deep draw to get the tobacco good and hot, thinking over what she'd heard. The women at dinner at the Mission, according to Louisine, had been perfectly cordial to Amelia, but reserved about George Reynolds. Out of courtesy or ignorance?

Mrs. Henrik, on the other hand, had let her tongue fly loose, flapping like the wings of that chicken on its last breath. A thieving interloper, she'd called him.

A Bitter Wind

The Whitneys were too kind to say anything truly harsh, but even they had allowed that perhaps the transaction involving the homestead was not what it appeared to be.

And the men in the saloon had suggested that Joe Bergen had not left the area, and that perhaps he drank and gambled.

Mary let her thoughts swirl and eddy like the river water, then float on by. When the tobacco had burned down and the dog had tired of chasing creatures who could fly out of his reach when they tired of the game, she pushed herself up and climbed the riverbank. There was one more man in Cascade who knew a thing or two. What he was willing to tell her might be another story.

She found the sheriff sitting at his desk, a letter spread out before him.

"Well, here I was enjoying a nice quiet afternoon and in you come," he said, but the way he said it, he didn't mean nothing by it. That first year Mary was living out at the Mission, he'd been downright hostile to her. When a killing happened nearby and he'd solved that problem and one of his own by arresting the town's only working woman, he hadn't taken kindly to Mary's interference. But she'd been right, both about the killer and his relationship with the lady in question, and he'd been man enough to admit it.

In the years since, he'd let on that he knew the tales people spun about her weren't necessarily true. Some folks didn't like her because she was Black. Some didn't like her because she carried a gun and knew how to use it. Some just plain didn't like her. All that meant nothing to her, long as they let her be. And most did. There had been that business with the neighboring ranch foreman over the harness, the last straw with the bishop in Helena, who'd made clear that Mother Amadeus had no choice but to send Mary away from the Mission.

But she'd learned a long time ago you couldn't do nothing about what other people thought or their talk. All that mattered was what you thought. You and the good Lord.

"Couldn't let you sit here with nothing to do, now could I?" Mary said. "You got to earn your keep, same as the rest of us."

His mustache twitched as he tried not to smile. Then he patted the letter. "I got plenty of work. What can I do for you, Mary?"

He didn't invite her to sit and she didn't. "I've been hearing some talk that worries me. You know anything about why Joe Bergen sold his place this past spring?"

The sheriff leaned forward, resting his arms on the edge of his desk.

"Now why do you want to be knowing about that?"

"He sold to a George Reynolds, originally from Pennsylvania and more recently from up near Great Falls. I delivered his intended bride, Amelia Morgan, out to the Mission to stay until their wedding, and I'm wondering what the girl's getting herself into, is all."

That wasn't all and she was sure he figured as much.

"Some men aren't cut out for the homesteading life," he replied.

"Joe Bergen one of 'em? His brother looks to be making it work. I seen his place. Cattle in the field and hay in the barn. Crops in the garden. Wife and a couple of kids, another on the way."

"Henrik's steady enough."

"His missus is of the mind that if Joe wanted to sell his place, he'd have sold to them. She—she used some unkind language about Mr. Reynolds and how he acquired the homestead. Any truth in it?"

"What kind of sheriff would I be if I didn't ask around

about a newcomer?"

But whatever he'd learned, the set of his face made clear he meant to keep it to himself.

"You check up on Amelia Morgan, too?"

His mustache twitched again. "I'll leave that to you, Mary."

"So where'd Joe take himself off to, then? Can you tell me that?"

He pushed back his chair and stood, a few inches taller than she. "Mary, I think it'd be better for you, and for the young lady, if you stopped asking questions."

"Just want to know if Joe Bergen's cleared out. Case he gets any mail."

"He get any mail before now?"

He had her there.

"Thank you kindly then." She reached for the brass door handle.

"Mary," he called, settling in his chair as she turned back to him. "You hear anything, you let me know."

She grunted and pulled the door hard behind her.

• • •

Mary didn't see Amelia or Louisine on her trips to the Mission that week or the next. Didn't see anyone useful—that is, anyone with anything to tell her. Though it had never been her way to poke into folks' personal business, she figured it wouldn't hurt nothing to be a tad bit nosy. Helpful. So as she worked her route, making deliveries and picking up mail, she asked the good folks of the community about some of their neighbors.

About Joe Bergen, she heard that he hadn't been seen here in weeks. Or maybe he'd been in the saloon, but that might have been his brother. They looked that much alike.

One heard he'd gone south to Helena, the capital, another east to Fort Benton, and yet another that he had a mining claim over near Belt. Mining wasn't what it used to be, but there were a few veins worth working. Or not. If Joe had experience in mining, no one could say.

Hadn't his family said California? You could take the Great Northern from Great Falls all the way to the coast these days, or ride the stage down to Butte and catch the Union Pacific.

About Mrs. Henrik, who'd voiced her complaints so fully, Mary heard little. The baby had not yet come, though from the size of the woman, any day now.

Nor could anyone say much about George Reynolds. He'd bought lumber and nails and other hardware, and hired a man to help him redig the well. He paid his bills on time and worked hard, and what more could anyone want? About his future bride, Mary heard that she was pleasant to visit with and fair enough to look at. Making herself useful to the sisters, though whether she was actually Catholic and when the wedding was to be, who knew? Did she know what she was getting into?

Did any woman? Any newcomer, for that matter?

The next Saturday, Mary kept a good pace on her route, to give her more time at the Mission. The grounds were quiet when she arrived. Change was coming. When the Jesuits left, now all but certain, the Indian boys would move on to other industrial schools run by the government, like the one at Fort Shaw. Some would leave school. A few of the settlers' sons might stay on, to be educated by the nuns, while others would ride into Cascade or board in town during the week. The sisters intended to keep the girls' schools open, despite the loss of the government contracts and the drop in the number of Indian students. It all meant more work for the sisters.

Plenty of truth in the old saying that life on the frontier was good for men and horses, but hard on women and cattle. The sisters would manage. Capable women, not given to complaints. Most of the time, that was. Mother Amadeus would expect nothing less. And Mary well knew how that good woman had a way of making you want to do what she expected of you.

She unhitched the team and set the horses loose in the corral to mingle with the day students' ponies and mares. She picked up the mailbag and started across the field.

"Mary!" She turned at the sound of her name. Amelia rushed toward her, in a black skirt and white blouse. "So good to see you. Let me take that."

"Watch yourself," Mary said. "It's heavy." But she handed the bag over and they walked together.

"You got a date for this wedding yet?"

"Soon, I think," Amelia said. "George wanted to put it off until the new roof is finished. The trip north put him behind, but all the plans are made for the cattle. They'll stay on the summer range for now and he'll bring them down in the fall. He and Benjamin."

"How you been keeping yourself busy?"

"A little sewing, a little reading. Mostly, though, I've been helping the sisters with the children. The schoolrooms are quite modern, filled with all the desks and slates and books you'd see back home. Even a piano."

Mary knew. She'd hauled most of it out here. Even the piano.

"I do think the girls ought all to be educated together and learn the same things," Amelia continued, "but no one seems to agree, so I keep my mouth shut. I always enjoyed my sisters' children. Babies are an awful load of work, but the older ones are so eager to learn. They are a true pleasure."

"Speaking of pleasures," Mary said. "How's that rose of yours growing?"

"George replanted it in an old washtub and took it to the cabin."

"Ain't that nice?"

They'd reached the school. Inside, in Amadeus's office, they sorted the mail. Most was for the Mother Superior, still away on her tour of the other schools. Correspondence from the bishops in Montana and Ohio, and the sisters back in Toledo. Letters requesting prayers and contributing funds. Funny how folks seemed to think money got a prayer answered faster. A few letters came for other sisters, including Louisine.

Nothing for Amelia. Mary hadn't seen one letter for her in all the time she'd been out here.

"Your family ain't big on writing, I take it," she said, stealing a quick glance at the younger woman and reaching for the short stack of letters ready to go.

"You know how farm life is, Mary. They have other things to do, but I know I'm in their hearts and prayers, as they are in mine."

Now that Mary thought about it, she'd only seen one letter from Amelia herself, to her father.

"So when's George figure to finish this new roof?"

"By the end of next week, he thinks. He and Thomas Whitney are at the homestead now. I have a letter and an apple butter pie for him, if you could swing by on your way back to town."

Considering what she'd heard about Joe Bergen, and her knowledge of single men living the farm and ranch life, Mary had to wonder if George Reynolds too took himself into town and gambled a bit when he was away from his home place. Nothing wrong with that. But it could lead to trouble.

"Amelia, don't mind me if it's none of my business, but you ask him about what Mrs. Henrik Bergen said that day my fool dog killed her chicken? Her words were mighty harsh."

"I did." Amelia cast her eyes down, then raised them. "He didn't want to tell me, but I pressed him. Said I had a right to know, after coming all this way to marry him."

"Good for him to know you got some backbone."

"Finally, he agreed. He met Joe Bergen in a saloon in Great Falls and heard that the man wanted to sell up. He says Joe wanted to move on, but never had the heart to tell his brother."

So instead Joe had left Henrik feeling that something that ought to have been his—at a fair price, if not a bargain—had been taken from him, leaving him to resent his neighbor and his brother.

Curious, after the two of them had made their way across the ocean and across the country together, staking claims side by side. Unless something else had come between them, but what could that be?

"He swears it's the truth," Amelia said.

Was it? Mary hoped so. The girl had come a long way on her own to settle in a new place, among new people. Hard enough, without neighbors holding grudges.

The school bell rang, followed almost immediately by shouts of children set free from learning for their midday meal and a bit of play.

"So now I know why Henrik's wife is angry," Amelia said as she and Mary walked to the cookhouse. "I wish I knew her name, but everyone calls her Mrs. Henrik. Apparently that's the custom in Norwegian families. But she should be angry with Joe, not George. It's Joe who didn't behave like family should."

Her voice trembled. Thinking of how her own family had

behaved, no doubt. Not making room for her at home or helping her find a situation close by, instead arranging for her to marry a man she scarcely knew in a place as foreign as if it had been Siberia or New Zealand.

"I can't shake the memory of her words," Amelia said.

Mary hadn't shaken them either. But she also hadn't learned anything to credit them, or explain them.

"The other neighbors are all pleasant enough," Amelia added. "Cautious, though. They liked Joe—or at least, they like Henrik, so they're willing enough to accept his brother, and if Henrik and his wife are unhappy with George, they're inclined to think there might be good reason. No one else has criticized him out loud, at least to my face. It's as if they want to wait, see what the truth is, before getting too friendly. See if we stick, as the homesteaders put it."

Mary bit her tongue, tasting the salt. See how the wind blows, more like.

Amelia went on. "I'm sure George has given no one reason to distrust him. But it's human nature to be resentful under the circumstances, isn't it? Back home, newcomers were sometimes treated with great suspicion."

"Oh, that's true all over," Mary said. "Of course, out here, everyone's a newcomer except the Indians and people treat them worst of all."

They'd reached the cookhouse and Amelia ducked inside for the pie. Then the two women walked toward the corral.

"You got to earn a place in people's respect," Mary said when they'd reached her wagon. "I'm sure you will, child. I'm sure you will."

Not until she and the team were back on the road did she realize not a word had been said about the wedding quilt.

• • •

A raven flew in front of her just before Mary steered the team toward the homestead. She crested the hill, staying left and glancing warily at the rutted track leading to Henrik Bergen's place. Any luck, that baby had come and Mrs. Bergen would not be out chasing her chickens and giving the postal driver a piece of her mind.

The cow and calf grazed in the field, alongside a horse she recognized as Thomas Whitney's and a sorrel she assumed belonged to George Reynolds.

The men had made good progress, the outside boards and the roof on the front of the addition about done. She heard the pounding of a hammer and peered up. A man straddled the ridge beside the stone chimney, only a leg visible from here. Who it might be, or where the other man was, she couldn't say.

Almost before she'd come to a stop, Jess leaped out of the wagon and sped toward the cabin, barking.

She set the brake and started to climb down. A gust struck her and she clamped a hand on her hat. Her foot slipped on the running board and she caught herself.

"Careful, you old woman," she muttered.

Both feet firmly on the ground, she reached into the wagon for the basket holding Amelia's pie, the letter on top. *George*, the envelope read, in a clear hand.

On the front porch stood the old washtub, the rose poking up, the cane greening nicely. The leaves that had been so tightly furled when Mary first saw the battered can carted all the way from Pennsylvania had grown larger and begun to open.

A speck of hope, in this troubling world.

A wooden chair stood beside the door. The hammering had stopped. Was that a shout she heard? She cocked her head. Two voices. More shouting. Then a clattering and a splintering, and a yell that about peeled her skin off.

Mary set the basket on the chair and hurried off the porch. The noise had come from out back and she followed it, struck by an eerie quiet.

Though as she rounded the corner of the cabin, all was not perfectly quiet. A swishing and a movement in the brush snagged her ear, coming from the hedge between the two homesteads. Jess on the trail of something? No. The big dog had come to her side, pushing and prodding, telling her to stop gawking, to get a move on.

But she had seen something. A child, a man? A shadow? She glanced up, expecting to see the raven again, or a hawk—a bird with wide wings making a pattern of light and dark that tricked you into thinking something was moving.

Nothing. Nothing but the wind that you couldn't see except by the ripples in the grass and the dirt it whipped up and blew into your eyes.

Another shout, another poke from the dog. Why had she left her rifle in the wagon? Because she was delivering a pie and a love letter, that was all. She followed Jess to the rear of the cabin.

"Good Lord!"

George Reynolds, whom she'd last seen leap easily over a young boy chasing after a rolling ball, lay in a heap on the ground, a broken ladder beside him. His leg was bent where it should have been straight and his moan was a terrible thing. She rushed toward him, seeing that one side of his face had been scraped red and raw, like a hog that had just been butchered. His blue shirt was torn, beginning to bloom red from a wound she couldn't see.

"Mary!"

She stopped. Who was calling her?

"Mary!" She heard her name again and looked up.

Thomas Whitney was clinging to the chimney with one arm, his other hand raised and bloodied.

"Help me get down."

She scanned the scene, spying the broken ladder on the ground. One side rail had snapped in two; the other was badly splintered. On the upper half of the ladder, several rungs had broken clear through.

"Turn it bottom side up," Thomas called from the roof, and she saw right away what he meant. But the broken half would only get in the way, making it impossible to use what remained in place.

She looked around for a saw. There must be a saw. Where had it gone to?

A few feet away, George moaned again.

Time was wasting. Mary put a foot on the side rail and reached for the broken piece.

"Careful now," she muttered to herself. "Ain't no time for you to break your neck."

She got a good grip. Put as much weight as she dared on the wood. Pulled, tugged, yanked, and twisted. Finally, the splintered rail broke free, the force of it considerable, but she kept her feet.

She dropped the useless section and dragged the other half of the ladder closer to the house. Raised it up. Not long enough to reach the eave, but it was as close as she could get.

"Can you slide down a ways, catch the ladder with your good hand?" she called. "I'll steady it best I can, once you get there."

She held her breath, one hand on her belly, and watched Thomas inch his way down the partly shingled roof, the heavy soles of his lumberman's boots keeping him from sliding clean off. He'd managed to wrap his handkerchief around his damaged hand, but even from the ground, she could see the blood seeping through. He tried once to use it to steady himself, but the cry of pain betrayed him.

Finally, his feet cleared the eave.

"Slow you now. It's a long reach to that first rung, and I can't be sure how solid it is. Move real careful like—"

Mary's heart pounded, sweat dripping into her eyes, as she talked the injured man down the damaged ladder. At last, one boot touched the ground, then the other, and Thomas nearly buckled in relief.

"What on earth—" she began, then stopped. No time to ask what had happened.

They turned their attention to George. The moans had stopped. Thomas knelt beside him, gently touching the broken leg with his good hand. The sink of his shoulders told Mary all she didn't want to know.

"Bad," she said. "I knew it. And that leg ain't his only injury. We got to get him to town, to the doctor." She could maneuver the wagon around back, but loading him by herself, with what little help the injured Thomas could give? Much as she prided herself on her strength, this was too much to manage without causing George more injury.

George moaned and turned toward her, his eyes glassy as he searched for hers, desperate to make contact.

"The ladder," he said. "Bergen . . ."

"Keep him comfortable. Staunch that blood if you can." She handed Thomas her handkerchief.

You up there, she said to herself, and hoped the good Lord was listening. *Whatever he done, he don't deserve this. Nor Thomas or Amelia neither.*

Then she steeled herself and made for the gap in the hedge.

"Wish I could, Mary," Henrik Bergen said a few minutes later, one beefy hand gripping the doorframe of his tidy white house. "I can help you load him, but I can't go into town with you. I can't leave my wife. I've sent my boy on horseback down to Mrs. Carlton. She did for my wife when the girl came along, and she's as skilled as any doctor."

As if summoned by his words, the little girl emerged from the shadows and stood beside him, clutching a scrap of cloth Mary guessed had once been her favorite blanket. Henrik reached down and cradled the back of her blond head in his big hand.

"Whatever you can do, then," Mary replied.

On their way back through the hedge, she glanced at Henrik's homestead cabin. Mrs. Henrik was lucky to have a safe, warm home and childbed, though plenty of women had given birth in shacks no bigger or better than the old cabin. A flour sack curtain hung in the open window, the front door ajar. Likely the children played out here and had left the door unlatched for a gust of wind to catch.

Lord knows there was plenty of wind in Montana.

She squinted. Was that a pair of boots beside it, one upright, one laying on its side?

Couldn't be. Shock of it all was making her see things.

Mary coaxed the team into pushing the wagon backwards between the cabin addition and corral, Henrik guiding them from the rear, all of them careful of the trees. Not big enough to give much shade, plenty big to get in the way. Henrik slid a board under George's broken body, and they loaded him into the back of the wagon, where Mary had used the blanket from the wagon seat to make a bed. She laid her oiled canvas slicker over him, then tucked her mailbag beneath his head. Jess jumped in and stretched out beside him, as if knowing his bulk would keep the man steady, his warmth keep him alive.

Henrik helped Thomas climb up onto the wagon seat.

Only then did Mary remember Amelia's basket.

"There's a pie sitting by the front door. You and your family ought to take it."

"That's mighty good of you," Henrik said. He held up one hand as she clucked to the team and drove slowly up the narrow track to the road.

"I tried to reach him," Thomas said when they'd left the homestead behind, his voice thin and broken. "George. When the ladder fell. It was windy. Caught my hand on—"

"Hush you," she said, though he was a grown man now and not the boy he'd been when they'd first met. "Save your strength." On these rutted, washboard roads, with the hard wagon seat beneath them, he was going to need it.

• • •

George Reynolds died two days later, Amelia Morgan and the doctor by his side.

"Don't you blame yourself now, Mary," the doctor told her later, on the porch outside his home, where he kept his medical office. "You got him here as quickly as you could."

"The rough ride didn't help none," she said.

"No, but that isn't what took him. He never had a chance."

Amelia was not so easily consoled. Mr. Whitney at the general store had sent a man out to the lumber mill to let his brother, father to Thomas, know of the young man's injury. On the way back, the courier had stopped by the Mission to get word to Amelia. She'd ridden in with him, not yet having a horse of her own. The doctor's wife had offered their spare bedroom, and she'd gladly taken it, spending every minute with George.

The doctor had repaired Thomas's hand as best he could,

but feared the bones and tissues would never fully heal. Thomas had chosen to stay with his aunt and uncle above the store, rather than return to his parents' home. He too visited George every chance he got.

George, and Amelia.

If George had spoken again, no one had told Mary, and she kept turning his last words to her over in her mind. She knew what she'd thought he meant at the time, the meaning she'd acted on, but what if . . .

No one knew how to get word of George's death to his brother. Benjamin Reynolds, General Delivery, Choteau, Montana, seemed most likely, but if he was a roaming cattle hand, it could be weeks before he went into town and got his mail. That town, anyway. Mary suggested they send similar letters to other towns as well.

The day after George's death, Amelia climbed into the wagon with Mary and Jess for the drive out to the Mission. When they neared the road to the homestead, she put a hand on Mary's arm.

"I want to see it. I want to see where it happened."

"Ain't nothing to see. Half-built house, half-broken ladder."

"That's as may be, Mary, but he did this for me, and I owe it to him to bear witness."

To what, Mary wondered. Whatever secrets the logs and lumber held, whatever tales the nails and hammers told, would have long blown away. But she gave the reins a tug and the team obeyed.

There was, as she had remembered, little enough to see. Henrik had taken care of the horses until they could be brought into the stables in Cascade, and he had charge and use of the cow and calf until other arrangements could be made. His own milk cow was old and he appreciated having a younger cow close to hand, even if most of her milk was going to the calf.

Mary drew the team to a halt.

Amelia kept her seat, hands gripped tight in her lap, and surveyed the place before speaking. "One thing I learned, when my mama and my brother died, is to face your grief and your tears straight on."

Then she climbed down, head high, and strode forward.

Jess, for once, stayed put. As if he remembered that there had been trouble the last time they'd been here and he thought Mary might need him again.

"Let her have a moment with her thoughts," she told him. Thoughts of the life she would have had on this homestead, memories of plans and dreams instead of what had been taken.

But after a few minutes, her stiff back got the better of her and she got to the ground. Clapped the side of her leg and Jess trotted alongside her. Someone had closed the front door. They walked around to the rear of the cabin. House. Whatever you called a place that was no longer one thing, not yet another. Somebody else would finish it, she supposed. Benjamin, if he wanted it. Or he'd sell the homestead to Henrik, who'd wanted it all along. What might become of the unfinished house then, no telling. But she was pretty sure that new stove and the fine curtains would make their way through the hedge to the white house.

The ladder remained where Mary had left it, one half propped against the back of the addition, the broken piece on the ground. There had been no rain since that day, and the patch of grass where George had fallen lay flattened, just as it had been. If she squinted, she could maybe see that some of the dirt was a shade darker than it ought to have been, from the blood.

All around were scuff marks and footprints. Hers and Thomas's, and Henrik Bergen's. And the sheriff's, when he rode out to size things up.

Mary stepped back for a better look, shading her eyes with her hand. The new house butted up along the chimney end of the cabin, the roof trimmed to make a tight fit. The chimney had been added on to, so it ran up alongside the new second story. Best she could figure, Thomas had been working on the ridge line, fitting shakes around the chimney stones. George had been working lower down—she could see a pile of shakes and a bag of nails right where he'd left them.

Everyone within thirty miles of Cascade was talking about the tragedy. If anyone thought there was anything suspicious about it, no one had said. Not in her hearing, anyway.

What Thomas had told the sheriff, when he was back in his right mind again, she didn't know. But she trusted her own ears and eyes. They told her someone else had been here. Someone who'd been arguing with George Reynolds, who'd walked away when he fell. Or who had helped him fall.

The thought gave her the prickles.

Be still, she told herself. Was someone watching her? Some folks swore you could tell, that you could feel eyes on you. Others called the notion pure nonsense. But at this very moment...

Slowly, she turned her head. In a gap in the lilacs stood the little girl, her eyes wide. Mary said nothing, and a moment later, the girl raised her hand, then disappeared through the hedge, out of sight.

"Well, I'll be," Mary said in a low voice, then made her way to the front. Amelia sat on the step beside the old wash tin, her basket at her feet.

"Someone watered the rose," she said. "And ate the pie,

but brought the basket and tin back. Even washed the cloth I used to line the basket."

"Forgot to tell you that. I told Henrik to take the pie. I imagine his wife saw to the washing."

"I hope she enjoyed the pie. I never wished her ill, despite what she said, and I choose to believe she did not truly wish ill on George or me. Besides," she said, a lightness in her voice that Mary had not heard in some time, "we didn't bring a gift for the baby. The pie will have to do."

Mary couldn't help let out a laugh.

"Though I would like to have my letter back," Amelia said.

Mary cursed herself. She'd plumb forgotten that Amelia had tucked a letter to George into the basket.

They made room for the rose in the back of the wagon. Poor thing. Come all this way, and now what? Amelia gave the place a long look, then climbed in and off they drove.

Neither woman spoke until well after they'd reached the road and turned toward the Mission.

"If only I hadn't insisted he find a place of his own," Amelia said.

"That don't make what happened your fault."

"Doesn't it? He would happily have found us lodgings in Great Falls and ridden out to work on someone else's farm or ranch, or found a job in town, if I hadn't been so stubborn. He would not have been up on that roof, determined to finish the house so we could get married. And Thomas wouldn't have been injured, either."

"You can't go thinking like that. None of us knows the good Lord's plans, but none of us can stop 'em from happening, whatever they might be."

They drove on, not speaking.

"I need to find Benjamin," Amelia said. "He needs to hear what happened from me."

"Nobody expects that of you."

"I expect it of myself. I owe it to George. Benjamin and I were all he had left. And our plans. Besides, the homestead is legally his, and the sooner he knows, the better. Will you take me to find him?"

Mary almost dropped the reins, the request astonished her so. Not that it would have mattered to the horses.

"Where you figuring to go? I got a route to keep."

"We can get there and back in a few days, I'm sure. Please, Mary."

"You been thinking about this."

"George said I thought too much."

"He might not have been wrong." In the distance, a hawk circled. "I suppose in those books of yours, when the man a woman's about to marry dies, she turns to his brother for comfort. Then the brother offers for her hand. And she marries him and they live happily ever after."

"In those books," Amelia said, "the woman has no other choice. I do."

• • •

At the Mission, they entrusted the rose to Louisine's care. Amelia collected a few things. If Amadeus were here, Mary might have gone to ask her opinion, but more than likely, she'd have said it's our duty to give help when it's in our power to do so.

Not that Mary needed anyone to tell her that.

Back in town, Amelia returned to the doctor's house for the evening. Mary went to see the sheriff.

"I rode out there," the sheriff said. He'd come in just ahead of her, and he set his peaked hat on his desk before resting one hip on the corner. His gun bumped against the desk, and he shifted the holster out of the way. "I walked around Reynolds's place. I talked to Henrik Bergen. He admits he was angry and insisted Joe try to get the place back. Both brothers talked to Reynolds, but he refused."

Mary let that sink in.

"I took a gander at that old cabin you mentioned," the sheriff continued. "Henrik says Joe did stay in it for a while, but that he's been gone for weeks now. Said he was leaving Montana and Henrik has no reason to think otherwise."

"Then why he get so hot when the men in the saloon claimed they saw Joe up in Great Falls? And now that George—" She stopped, pressed her lips together, and shook her head. "Henrik don't want nobody thinking that brother of his been anywhere near George Reynolds."

The sheriff spread his hands. "For all I know, the ladder blew over in the wind, right as George was climbing down. You speculating otherwise doesn't change anything."

"I know what I heard. No speculation about it. I heard an argument. Now maybe Thomas can't say one way or the other—"

"Thomas didn't see anyone. He thought he heard voices. You thought you heard voices. But neither of you knows for sure that anyone else was there."

"What about what George said? Don't we credit a dying man?"

"George said 'the ladder' and Bergen's name. He could've been telling you to go next door and ask Henrik Bergen for help. That's what you thought at the time."

He was right. That's what she'd thought and what she'd done. Not until later had she started to wonder otherwise.

"Now, Mary," he said, eyeing her as he pushed himself to standing. "I don't want to hear any more about this. We got no reason to accuse Joe Bergen of causing George Reynolds harm or Henrik of covering up for him. Henrik's a good man."

But she couldn't shake the memory of Henrik's anger. The boots on the cabin porch. The boy wanting to fetch someone. His uncle, she'd been sure. She was still sure.

And the shadow in the hedge after George's fall. The shadow she hadn't mentioned to anyone. But she'd seen it. She knew she'd seen it.

"I don't expect you to be convinced, Mary," the sheriff said. "Hell, I'm not half convinced myself. But even if I could find the man, I got no evidence of a crime."

And there was nothing more she could say to that.

• • •

Mile after mile, the women drove through the open country. Not a farm or ranch in sight. They drove through wild grasslands where antelope grazed, the breeze rippling the grasses and anything else it could find. They crested a small ridge and Amelia pointed, wordless, at a giant hawk circling above the land, head bowed, eyes sharp. The circles grew smaller, the hawk slowly dropping closer to the ground. What was it watching, what was it waiting for? Then it dove, sharp and sudden, snatching something they couldn't see with its powerful talons.

Amelia shuddered. Mary kept a grip on Jess.

Life and death went hand in hand, no matter how much you wanted to forget it.

At one point, they caught a glimpse of the mountains rising up in the west. The Rockies. Real mountains, not like the squared-off buttes and craggy hills that dotted the land around them.

After a few miles, they spotted a narrow stream and stopped to let the horses drink the cold mountain runoff.

They filled their water jug and sat by the side of the stream to eat a bit of the bread and jam they'd brought.

The food gone, but her bones not quite ready yet to pick up and move on, Mary asked the question that had been bothering her.

"Why you so keen on finding this Benjamin?"

Amelia didn't answer and Mary wondered what muck she'd accidentally stuck her foot in.

"I told you," Amelia said after a long while, "that my mother died from the flu, and my brother three days later."

She paused, though whether to choose her words or out of regret for starting down this path, Mary couldn't guess.

"What I didn't say, because it didn't matter to the telling then, but now it does, is that I was away helping a cousin with a new baby. She'd been ill through most of her pregnancy and her husband was struggling to take care of the two older children. They needed an extra pair of hands and I was glad to be of use." Another silence. "Nobody told me what happened. No one wrote or sent word. Not until weeks later, when I got home . . ."

"Oh, child. You came home to the terrible news." Not only had she learned she'd lost the two people she'd loved most. She'd learned that those left behind had spared little thought or regard for her.

That said more about why she left Pennsylvania than any wooing by mail ever could.

"I decided then that I would never let anyone suffer as I had. That I would choose who to love and how to live. But it isn't so easy, is it, Mary?"

Mary reached out and took the girl's hand. Squeezed it and didn't let go, not until the girl squeezed back, her eyes damp, her mouth tight, and nodded quickly. Then it was time to get a move on.

Soon after, they reached the town of Fort Shaw. The fort itself, south of town, had closed a few years back, the buildings now housing the boarding school the government ran for Indian children. Mary had visited once when the soldiers of the 10th Cavalry, the Buffalo Soldiers, first arrived. My, but it had been good to see Black faces.

Mary drove the wagon down the main street.

"Good heavens," Amelia said. "I didn't think a town could be much smaller and dustier than Cascade. Hard to imagine Benjamin spending much time here."

"What do you know about the man?"

"Not much. I never met him. He's two years older than George. They came West together. George said Benjamin preferred life on the range to life in town. I don't expect he'll want to keep the homestead, unless he's had a change of heart."

"Happens," Mary said. "'Specially as a man gets older, and if he wants a wife."

"I imagine the postmaster should be our first stop."

"Ain't no post office," Mary said. "Closed when the soldiers left. A driver rides the route, same as me, but he won't be so easy to find."

"The mercantile then." She pointed to the general store, a small frame building easily identified. "Unless . . ."

Unless Mary didn't think she'd be welcome, Amelia didn't say. Most of the white settlers had tolerated the Buffalo Soldiers well enough, aside from the incident not long after they arrived at Fort Shaw in 1888 that led to a lynching. They were soldiers, doing their duty putting down Indian rebellions and miners' strikes, and whites were grateful enough for that. Besides, soldiers were never expected to stay put for long. None had stayed here, far as she knew, though a handful had settled in Great Falls.

"You go ahead," Mary said, bringing the team to a stop. "I got my eye elsewhere."

Amelia glanced at the saloon across the street, then at Mary, a sly glimmer in her eye. Once on the ground, she dusted off her skirt, strode to the general store, and pushed open the door.

Mary felt her bones creak as she climbed down from the wagon. Shot of whiskey would do her good.

The man behind the bar was polishing a glass when she entered. Barkeepers were always polishing something, though by the looks of this place, there weren't much else to do. Two men sat at a round table, a bottle and two glasses between them, cards in hand. No money on the table. This saloon didn't look as prosperous as the one in Cascade. Not nearly as many bottles on the backbar, the woodwork much less ornate. But the mirror was big enough for a view of the goings-on.

Mary strode to the bar. "Mary Fields," she said. "From Cascade. Passing through, and a little dry. Shot of whiskey, if you've got one."

"I do," the bartender said, setting a glass in front of her. He reached beneath the bar and brought out a bottle. Poured a decent measure and slid the glass toward her.

She let it sit a moment, until the sounds of cards being dealt resumed. She pulled the glass closer and raised it. Smelled good, like fruit and grain and oak. She took a sip, then nodded.

"Hits the spot."

"Glad to hear it. What brings you to Fort Shaw?"

"Looking for a man named Benjamin Reynolds," she said. "Bringing news of his brother. Any chance you know where I might find him?"

"Ben? Haven't seen him in quite a spell," the bartender said. "Not bad news, I hope."

"'Fraid so."

The place was quiet enough, and small enough, that the card players heard the exchange.

"Reynolds?" the man in the brown coat and vest said. "I think he's working up north."

"His brother George?" the other man asked.

"That's the one," Mary said.

"No surprise," he replied.

But that was all he said. And if the bartender had heard talk about George Reynolds, he wasn't spreading it.

Amelia had done a mite better squeezing details out of the shopkeeper. Benjamin Reynolds had last been in the general store several weeks ago. Got his mail there, even though the town no longer had an official post office. No telling when he might come in—late spring was busy in the cattle business. Cattle to round up and count, calves to ready for branding and knifing. Fences to mend. He'd given her the name of the rancher Benjamin last worked for and rough directions. Of George, he claimed to know nothing.

They decided to push on. They crossed the Sun River and drove up a long slope. Near the base of another butte, the gray-brown rock resembling columns that had been mashed together, scrubby pines sprouting from the cracks, the road forked. Mary looked at Amelia.

"West, I think," Amelia said, answering the unasked question. "The shopkeeper talked with his hands and I got confused. I should have asked him to draw a map. Why don't I hike up the hill a bit and see what lies beyond?"

Jess went with her, jumping down easily. Funny how the prospect of a run with a new friend loosened his stiff old joints.

Mary stayed put, grateful for the chance to study the land stretching out around them. A place of perfect emptiness and freedom. Empty didn't mean blank. It meant it could be what you wanted—well, you couldn't never make this into a cotton field, not with all that sagebrush and not near enough water. You couldn't always make the life you wanted—it got snatched away sometimes, like it had for Amelia. Twice now, despite her being so young.

But you could make your own self into what you wanted.

Mary had been wrong about Amelia. Oh, she'd understood the girl was a castoff, one too many in a family that could barely take care of itself, let alone an unattached female. But she'd been wrong in thinking Amelia had chosen marriage to a near-stranger in search of a life like the one she'd been denied back East.

No. Amelia had not known what the land out here would be like, true. And she hadn't known George Reynolds all that well—or maybe not as well as she should have.

She'd come West not to escape, but for the freedom to choose her own life. And now she was choosing to act with an open heart, when no one would have blamed her for being angry and resentful and full of spite.

Only problem with this land was you couldn't always find a place to answer nature's call without being seen. As if there was anyone to see her.

Mary spotted a big gray rock and took herself to the far side, away from the rutted track they'd been driving. Hitched up her skirt and spread her legs, lowering her bulk.

And heard a sound that sent her flying high and off on a run faster than she'd run in forty years. She jerked the pistol out of her pocket, and when she'd reached a safe distance, turned and aimed.

The rattler remained coiled, its head high above the grasses. Damned if those beady eyes weren't looking straight at her.

She fired once. A puff of dust and pieces of snakeskin

flew up and drifted back down to the earth.

She heard a shout and saw Amelia running down the hillside, the dog racing beside her.

"Mary, what is it?"

"Settle down, child," Mary called, the pistol steady in her hand. Startled, Amelia followed her gaze, then covered her mouth with her hand.

The two women and the dog lost no time clambering into the wagon. Mary pulled out the water jug and took a long drink, then handed it to the girl.

They followed the road as it led on, north by northwest. It was dry, deeply rutted in some places, carved by channels water had left behind in others. Mary was getting old for journeys like this. Made her a mite uncomfortable to miss her mail route, but any luck, they'd be back before anyone noticed. If folks complained—well, that was folks for you. They were waiting on something, they could go into Whitney's general store and pick it up themselves.

Besides, it was good to get away, to do something for someone else. With someone else.

The trip had her thinking about choices. Weren't just people like her who'd had choices taken away from them for so long. A woman wanted to be in charge of her own life, she didn't have a lot of options. The convent. Teaching, though in some places a woman had to give that up when she married. Homesteading on your own—women had done it. Took grit and maybe a bit of foolishness.

Who was she, calling anyone else foolish?

"How can such a bitter wind blow while the sun shines?" Amelia shivered and tugged on her coat.

Mary had no answer, intent on her driving.

They spotted a small log cabin down by a creek, but the horses had a few more miles in them, so they kept going.

They had food, and a canvas tarpaulin, and as they got closer to the mountains, the creeks and streams were more plentiful. They could make do when they were ready.

"Look!" Amelia said a few minutes later, pointing at the skies darkening in the west. "That storm's rolling in out of nowhere."

Mary cursed herself. She should have known better, letting herself get lost in her own imaginings and not watching the sky. She yanked her slicker out from under the wagon seat and pulled it on, shifting the reins from one hand to the other.

"Keep an eye out for a place to shelter," she told Amelia. "Best to get close to a stream, with tall shrubs or trees to protect the horses."

No sooner had she spoken than an eddy of dust and dirt swirled in front of them, striking her face and stinging her eyes. She snatched off her hat and shoved it beneath her thigh, then hung on to the reins with both hands.

Amelia let out a cry and shielded her eyes. The horses had slowed, and Peter balked, shaking his mane to chase the dust away.

"Up there," Mary said, squinting as the rain began to hit them. How the air turned so wet so fast, coming at them like buckshot and filling the rivulets in the road, she didn't know, but that's how it was sometimes in this country. "That a homestead?"

"Yes, I think it is," came Amelia's muffled reply.

And just in time, as the rain became sleet. But not, it turned out, the most hospitable of homes.

The ranch wife had seen them coming, pulling on an oilskin slicker as she came out the front door of a low-slung log house and scurried toward the barn, bare head bent against the rain.

"Put your horses in here," she called. "Wagon too, if you don't want to be up to the hubs in mud. There's hay and water aplenty, and I've got last Sunday's ham hock flavoring a bean stew. Won't take me no time to make up some cornbread."

The moment Mary heard the woman's accent, she knew the welcome would be taken back as soon as the woman saw her face. So it came as no surprise, when they were safely inside the barn, that the ranch wife offered Amelia a bed in the house, then spoke to Mary.

"I imagine you'd be more comfortable out here," she said.

I'd be more comfortable home in my own bed, Mary thought, *a damn sight warmer and more comfortable than yours.*

"We'll both sleep out here," Amelia said. "Keep the road dust and mud off your floors. We've packed plenty of food, of course, but since we can't very well build a fire, we'd sure appreciate some of that soup. And the cornbread."

After the horses were unhitched and watered, Jess scurried around the barn, which wasn't very big but had a sound roof, and declared it safe, despite the presence of a milk cow and a swayback mare. Amelia crossed the small farmyard to the house. Mary took off her coat, grateful to have gotten it back after she delivered George to the doctor's office, and laid it over the side of the wagon to dry. Leaned her rifle against a wheel. Made herself a chair out of straw, loosened her boots, and settled in.

"Bones," she muttered. "Don't give out on me now."

Amelia entered the barn, carrying a basket that held a small kettle of soup and generous squares of cornbread, along with fresh butter and a pot of wildbee honey. They dug bowls and spoons out of the grub box and tucked in.

"I wish you'd brought that jug of yours, Mary," Amelia said when they were finished.

"And here I was wishing you'd brought one of those apple butter pies of yours."

The next morning, the skies were clear, the ground that had been soaked the night before now nearly bone-dry again. The air smelled clean, as though refreshed by the storm.

Amelia returned from the ranch house with the basket, full once again.

"Bread and jam," she said.

"We got our own," Mary said. The straw bed had done well enough, and the soup had been warm and welcome. They'd been lucky to find a roof at all. Even so, it stung to be told, by actions if not words, that she didn't belong out here. And no telling what today might bring.

"But we don't have this." Amelia pulled a heavy tin coffeepot out of the basket and the scent almost overpowered the smell of horse, cow, hay, and manure that permeated the barn. "Toasted grains, with a few real coffee beans thrown in. I think she felt badly for how she treated you."

As she should have, but Mary didn't bother saying so.

"I asked her where we might find this ranch where Benjamin works." Amelia filled their tin cups. "She drew the brand in the top of the flour bin. Do you know, I suspect she can't read. Anyway, it's most of a morning's drive. We watch for an old snag, a pine tree struck by lightning, and go right. Her husband's hired on there for a bit, even though his being away means falling behind on their own work. But it's cash pay, and you can't say no to that."

The coffee wasn't half bad. Cash pay meant money for real beans now and then, and she couldn't begrudge the woman that, could she?

"I reckon she'd like you to stay on a bit, for some woman talk."

"She said as much, but I explained that we needed to deliver some news. Precisely what and why, I kept to myself."

Mary and Jess took the horses down to the stream while Amelia repacked their grub box and took the coffeepot and basket back to the ranch house. Team hitched, they drove north.

Amelia had grown oddly quiet.

"You worrying what to say to him? He's a grown man. He'll think what he's gonna think."

"I've never had to break bad news like this."

Though she'd received plenty of it, and never in a good way.

"Says well of your heart that you want to cushion the blow, but he's gonna hear one way or another, and better from someone who loved his brother than in a letter." Mary gave her a sidelong look. "You ain't still thinking George's death is your fault, are you?"

"I made up my mind to love him and I truly did," Amelia said. A curl had come loose from her hair, but she didn't seem to notice. "I'm not the only one who thinks I'm to blame for his death. I've heard the talk, at the Mission and in town. Mrs. Henrik wasn't the only one. They're right, you know. I did refuse to marry him until he found the farm we'd dreamed of. Now they're saying . . ." She let the sentence drift on the air.

"What? That George shouldn't have taken what Joe Bergen offered? That's bitterness talking." Those same women knocking at Amelia's insistence that George be settled before she married him would all scoff at her if she wed a man who couldn't support her. Willing to say one thing when it suited them and swing all the way 'round to the opposite another time.

But talk aside, there was something about all this that she couldn't quite work out.

"I wish I could be so sure," Amelia said. "As well as I thought I knew George, I didn't know everything, as he didn't know everything about me. Benjamin will have every right to be angry with me. Maybe I should have been content to send the news by letter."

"Man ain't too quick to pick up his mail," Mary said, and Amelia let out a small, wry laugh.

There was no turning back now.

"Seems like north never ends out here," Amelia said after a distance.

But not much later, she spotted the brand the ranch woman had drawn in the flour. It was burned into a pine lintel mounted over the entrance to a narrow but well-worn drive. The horses trotted down the draw to ranch headquarters, a cluster of cow sheds and hay barns, a long, low bunkhouse, and a fine two-story clapboard house with a covered porch on two sides. Its steeply pitched roofline gave Mary the shudders. Amelia, too, if she read the girl's posture right. Then Amelia straightened her shoulders and tightened her jaw, steeling herself against the memory of a steep roof's dangers.

Mary did the same.

Luck was with them. The first ranch hand they spoke to said Benjamin Reynolds was in the far corral, working with a young bronc. He could go find the man or tend to their team if they wanted to search him out themselves. Mary looked to Amelia. Her pledge, her choice.

"If you'd be so kind," Amelia said, making to rise. The man helped her down. She glanced back at Mary, who understood. She'd stay put. Jess, though, made up his own mind and trotted after the girl and the ranch hand.

It wasn't long before she returned, and if Mary hadn't seen the broken body of George Reynolds herself, she'd have thought it was him walking beside Amelia. Benjamin was as tall as his younger brother, with the same confident stride. The same tilt of the head and shoulders as he listened, then spoke.

"Your reputation precedes you, Miss Fields," he said, holding out his hand when Amelia made the introduction. No ghost he, but flesh and blood. "For delivering the mail on time, battling wolves and bishops and blizzards."

"Nonsense," she said. Was the easy talk meant to charm her or to hide his pain? "But I am sorry about the news we brought."

He let out a long sigh, and brushed his hand across one eye, drawing his palm down his cheek. "Thank you. I do appreciate you and Miss Morgan making the trip. As you discovered, I don't go into town too often. Some mail finds me here at the ranch, but then, you wouldn't have known that. I hadn't gotten around to letting my brother know I'd come back to the ranch as foreman, and that I intend to stay."

Amelia's eyes showed her surprise. "But he was just here two weeks ago, on his cattle-buying trip. That trip delayed work on the house, and our wedding."

"I'm afraid you're mistaken," Benjamin said. "I haven't seen George since last winter. We met up in Great Falls to mark the new year."

"But—but he told me." Amelia turned to Mary, confused. She caught her lower lip between her teeth, then spoke to Benjamin. "He told me he'd gone north to scout some cattle, and that he'd seen his brother on the trip. He said he spent the night with you."

If she'd expected Benjamin to correct himself, to say he'd been mistaken, yes, of course he'd seen George not two weeks ago, she was disappointed.

"Did he come home trailing cattle?" Benjamin asked.

"No-o-o. He said—" Amelia furrowed her brow, searching her memory for details crowded out by all that had happened since. "He said the two of you would bring them down this fall."

"I've shocked you, and I'm terribly sorry. Perhaps you'll sit and let me try to clear up your confusion." He gestured to the porch, where a pair of spindle-backed wooden chairs sat at either end of a long bench that put Mary in mind of a church pew. "You, too, Miss Fields."

Amelia mounted the wide porch steps alongside Benjamin. Mary followed. The invitation suggested that he was held in high regard on the ranch, or that he didn't mind being too familiar.

Amelia sank into one of the wooden chairs while Mary settled herself on the bench. The door to the house opened and a slender woman in a high-necked white dress emerged.

"Benjamin?" she said, and her tone told Mary why Benjamin Reynolds had decided to stay.

"Darling," he said, "I've had some bad news."

"About George?"

He nodded and she took his hand, keeping hold of it as she slipped into the closest chair. He made the introduction. Miss Catherine Ruston, his fiancée. Something else Amelia had not known, judging by the way her fair skin grew even paler.

Benjamin relayed the bare facts of George's death on the homestead outside Cascade.

"Benjamin," Catherine Ruston said. "You need to tell Miss Morgan what you've told me."

He pressed his lips together and closed his eyes briefly, then nodded. "They say you shouldn't speak ill of the dead, and I hate to cause you any more distress. But I'm afraid my brother was not all he seemed to be. He told you he'd come up this way to buy cattle, but I believe he was in Great Falls, at the card table."

Dark spots appeared on Amelia's cheeks.

"There's nothing wrong with a game of cards now and then. Even a friendly wager, though the government may say otherwise." His lips curved briefly, without humor. "The problem is when a man uses his own wits and skill to take advantage of another man."

"Are you telling me I was engaged to marry a gambler? A card shark or a con man?" Amelia straightened, practically spitting out the words. "Mr. Reynolds, I do not believe you."

"No, no." He held out his hands. "Not so low as that, Miss Morgan. I'm saying George knew how to press an advantage when it presented itself. I believe that may have been how he acquired the cabin and acreage, and that he may have gone back to the card table to try to win money to buy those cattle. They don't come cheap. My brother and I have had to work to support ourselves since we were barely more than boys. He had more brains than most—certainly more than I do." Another quick smile. Though his features were much like his brother's, Benjamin Reynolds had a different air about him. A kinder spirit, perhaps.

"But sometimes," he finished, "George pressed his advantage when it would have been wiser to hold back."

"The Bergens are right," Amelia said to Mary. "George won the homestead off Joe. No wonder they hated him, and they hate me. I'm the one who pushed him, saying I wouldn't marry him until he was settled." Wild-eyed, she turned to Benjamin. "Forgive me."

"Nothing to forgive, Miss Morgan. My brother, if the stories are to be believed—and I do believe them—saw this man Bergen's weakness. I'm not saying he cheated. But he knew Bergen wasn't a good player, maybe a little worse for drink, and took him up on a game anyway. The man got in over his head and offered the deed to the property. Some men would walk away at that point. George did not. He waited for the man to make a mistake, and it was a big one."

"You sound pretty sure of all that," Mary said. If George had gambled since his move to Cascade, they'd have heard the talk sooner. She would have heard it. But no. He'd chosen not to engage in scandalous—or illegal—behavior so close to home. Was it worse to be caught by the devil of greed, or to deliberately choose to use your skill against one with less of it?

"It's how he won our train fare out here seven years ago," Benjamin said. He'd moved to stand behind his fiancée's chair, hands resting on its carved back. "It's what he always did when he needed more than wages. But I'm not just guessing. I saw his habits myself, at the new year, and I heard the story from a man who saw the game with this Bergen. He heard George say now he could get married. I didn't know he was courting. If I had—" He spread his hands. But what could he have done?

"I am so sorry, Mr. Reynolds," Amelia said, "to have forced you to tell me all this. I believed your brother loved me."

"I have no doubt," he said quickly. "He did not have a cruel heart. Despite what I've said, I have nothing but fondness for him. And I don't blame you. Accidents happen. Please don't fault yourself."

But had it been an accident? Mary kept her wonderings to herself.

It was decided that Benjamin would ride back to Cascade with Mary and Amelia, leaving early the next morning. He judged that they could make the trip in one day, taking a shorter route that would bypass the small ranch where they'd spent the night.

"We have only one spare bedroom," Miss Ruston said, glancing from Amelia to Mary, "quite small to share. We do have the homestead shack. It's quite habitable, I assure you."

Amelia opened her mouth, ready to protest, but Mary held out a hand. "You stay in the house. The shack will do for me and Jess, long as Miss Ruston and her folks don't mind me having a smoke."

"No one will mind at all," came the reply. In truth, the shack was almost as big as her house in Cascade, and just as clean. And a few hours to herself in a place near a stream soothed her soul.

The weather held and Mary was grateful. Doing good deeds was sometimes hard on old bones. Benjamin rode his big bay ahead of the wagon, as he knew the road, and they made good time. They stopped near a stream to let the horses rest, and Amelia slipped into the dense brush. Mary stood beside the wagon, hands on her hips, and arched her back.

"Miss Fields," Benjamin said. "What can you tell me about these Bergens?"

"Not much to tell. Joe and Henrik are brothers, come from Norway. Homesteaded side by side. Both proved up, but Henrik's done more to his place than Joe did. He's got a wife and a couple of young'uns. Plus a new baby."

"Do they know how Joe lost his deed?"

Jess pressed against her leg and she rubbed his head, glad for the comfort he gave. "Mrs. Henrik is mighty angry. She'd like to have that place for her family, but whether she thinks Joe sold out on his own or fell prey to another man's greed, I couldn't say. They been telling everyone he's gone to California. It's not up to me to say whether that's the truth."

"I hear the farming's a lot easier out there."

"But you got to deal with a lot more people," Mary said, and Benjamin chuckled, then turned to face her, his expression serious.

"You know this territory. You know Amelia and you know the Bergens. What would you suggest I do?"

She gazed around the vast, open space, the big sky. After a long moment, she spoke. "Once a land got a taste of people, it don't want to sit empty, do it?"

Benjamin said nothing. Then they heard the rustle of leaves and skirts, and Jess dashed off into the spring green brush to escort Amelia back to the wagon.

• • •

"Hold your horses. I'm coming." Whoever was pounding on her door so early in the morning it might as well be night?

"'Morning, Mary," the sheriff said when she opened the door, still in her nightdress, a shawl around her shoulders. "Sorry to disturb you, but I have need of you and your wagon."

"Good Lord. Not another accident?"

"'Fraid it's worse than that."

Joe Bergen, whose family had been telling everyone who'd listen that he'd gone to seek his fortune in California, had been found. Found facedown in a slough the other side of the river. Single set of footprints that looked like the boots on his feet. No signs of a struggle in the slippery mud. There was little question that he'd taken his own life.

Mary sat in the wagon, unlit pipe in hand, as the sun finished rising. The sheriff, the farmer who'd spotted the body, and another man fished it out and hauled it up the bank. Once the wagon was loaded, she drove to the jail and around the back, while one of the men went for the doctor.

"Soon as Doc's seen the body and we've tucked it in a cell to keep cool," the sheriff said while they waited, "I'll ride over to Henrik's place."

"So much for them saying he went out to the coast."

"I should have believed you, Mary, when you told me he was hiding in Henrik's homestead cabin."

"Something else you should know," she said, and recounted Benjamin Reynolds's belief that George had acquired the deed to the homestead in an illegal game of cards. The sheriff listened attentively.

"I had heard talk about that, but no one came forward to say for sure. I suspect Henrik had an idea, but speaking up would have implicated his brother just as much as Reynolds."

"And you know what else people will say." She folded her arms across her chest and met his gaze.

"That Joe Bergen might as well have stood on the jailhouse steps and declared he killed George Reynolds." The sheriff blew out a noisy breath. "Should have believed you about that, too."

"Gives me no pleasure to be right about a man's death. Two deaths. But it were the only way things made any sense."

At Mary's suggestion, the sheriff summoned Benjamin from the hotel where he'd taken a room after their late arrival and the two men rode out to break the news together. Amelia had spent the night at the doctor's house, and found Mary at the stables.

"It's true, isn't it?" she said as soon as she saw Mary's face. "Joe Bergen did away with himself. Was he that ashamed of losing the deed to George in a card game?"

"No, child. I don't think so. Gambling's been illegal since statehood, but it happened anyway and it weren't that big a sin." Mary wiped a hand across her forehead. It had been a long day already and she hadn't had her breakfast. Cup of strong coffee would do her good, along with a thick slice of bread and butter and a dab of that crab apple jelly.

"Some believe taking one's own life is a sin."

"They do. And everybody agrees taking another man's life is a sin."

"Whatever do you mean?"

"I mean I don't think it was an accident that George came off that roof. I think Joe confronted him—sheriff says it weren't the first time—and raised a fuss. He wanted to buy the property back and George refused."

"Because of me."

"Because he was one of those men who thinks he can outwit others, without it catching up to him. That day at the homestead, Joe was yelling up a ruckus. Thomas heard it. So did I, though neither of us knew who it was. George had started down the ladder when it broke and he fell, same time as Thomas lost his hold on the chimney, trying to keep George from falling. What I think is Joe Bergen pushed that ladder."

Amelia held her steepled hands to her lips. "And when Joe saw what had happened, he ran off."

"I could never say for sure it was him I saw bolting through the bushes, but it mighta been. Had to have been. Thomas didn't see—not from where he was and all the noise he was making, hammering away."

Amelia slumped against a post. "Suicide. Some call it weakness or cowardice. I don't know about that, but causing serious harm to a man and refusing to stay and help him is heartless and cruel."

"It is that," Mary agreed. "As for throwing himself in the river, some will say he wasn't in his right mind. Others think a man's got a right to decide for himself when he's done with this life."

"What do you think, Mary?"

"I think Joe Bergen blamed your George for his own mistakes, to avoid having to face the consequences of what he done. He nursed his anger till it got the best of him and he made it worse, then he couldn't live with what he'd done."

He'd chosen his own consequences. Did a man have that right, or was he obliged to stay alive and accept the consequences society and the law imposed on him? Either way, he would ultimately face God's judgment. And no one alive could say what that might be.

"I expect you're right," Amelia said. "Except he's not my George. He's not—he wasn't—the man I thought he was."

"I expect what hit him the hardest was realizing he wasn't the man he wanted to be, especially once you arrived and he got to know your heart from your actions and not just your pretty letters."

Amelia let that sink in. "Thank you, Mary. You've been nothing but kind to me, you and the sisters."

"I'm right glad to hear you feel that way. Your welcome to Montana's been pretty rough."

Though Mary would have liked little better than a day fussing with the peonies and iris beginning to bloom outside her front door, the mail had waited too long already and she would not shirk her responsibility.

"No rest for the wicked, eh, boy?" she muttered to the dog as she hoisted the mailbag into the wagon. Then she patted her pocket to make sure the surprise she'd tucked in it earlier was still there.

She'd offered to take Amelia with her out to the Mission, but the young woman chose to stay in town another day, to rest in the care of the doctor's wife. Lord knew, it would be harder for people to spread rumors about her if she were right there in town for everyone to see.

When she neared the homestead, Mary hesitated a moment before pointing her team down the narrow track. The sheriff came riding toward her, alone. He pulled up alongside the wagon.

"Hardest part of the job," he said, with a tight jaw and a quick shake of his head. "Thank you again, Mary, for helping out this morning." He raised his hat, bid her a good day, and rode on.

At the fork, she steered the horses left, and the cabin and its unfinished addition soon came into view. Benjamin's horse grazed nearby, but there was no sign of the man.

She and Jess found him out back, perched on a stack of shakes, running the brim of his hat through his long fingers.

"Miss Fields." He stood. "You can almost feel the sadness here, can't you?"

The sadness of a life gone to waste and what it took with it. In her long years, Mary had seen many a life end sooner than it should have, and others stunted for as many reasons as there were stories. Sadness was shifty that way. It could hide in the green grass and the young leaves, the sparrow's song and the raven's wing. Happiness hid there, too. It all depended on how you saw it.

"I believe you and the sheriff have the right of it," he said, looking from the broken ladder to the damaged roof. "Though I can't think Bergen planned to push the ladder, or that he meant to cause my brother serious harm. And he certainly couldn't have meant for Thomas Whitney to lose part of the use of his hand."

Thomas, as innocent in all this as Amelia, despite what the girl thought about her own part.

"I've been thinking about what you said, yesterday at the stream," Benjamin continued. "That once land's been touched, it doesn't like to sit empty."

Mary tilted her head, waiting for him to finish his thought.

"Can you spare a few more minutes? I have a proposal for Mr. Bergen, and if you're there as my witness, I'm less apt to lose my nerve."

They walked around the front of the cabin, where Mary filled a bucket of water for her team. Then they crossed the open field and rounded the hedge. Now that it was in full leaf, Mary couldn't see the cabin in back, where Joe Bergen had taken refuge. Probably better that way.

Henrik sat on his porch, rocking. The boy stood beside him. When he grew up, would he take after the father he adored, or the uncle he'd loved? No telling yet.

"Mr. Bergen, I'm Benjamin Reynolds."

"I know who you are."

"My condolences on the loss of your brother."

Henrik's jaw twitched. "And mine on yours."

"I understand that your brother attempted to buy the deed to the homestead back, after it was lost."

"He did, and I made an offer myself, but we were refused."

"I'm wondering if you and I can do a little business." He set one foot on the step and leaned forward, forearm to knee. "I'm putting down roots elsewhere, and Miss Morgan does not care to run the homestead on her own. As I've heard the story, the deed was offered as ante, but no one's been able to tell me how much money was at stake."

"Shouldn't have been any money at stake. The game was illegal. My brother played of his own will, but he was expecting a friendly game. He didn't expect to run into a man of your brother's skill."

"I'd say, Mr. Bergen, that when your brother decided to place everything he owned on the line, he took the game well beyond what you might call friendly."

Mary watched the two men stare at each other. Calling each other's bluff, they were, without a deck of cards in sight. Who had the ace? Who had the heart?

Finally, a bit of color rising in his face, Henrik Bergen reached for his boy. "I don't have much cash money."

"I don't need much. I only want to make sure that Miss Morgan can return to Pennsylvania if she cares to, or get settled somewhere else of her choosing."

The two men discussed what George had spent on lumber and roof shakes and the new stove, and settled on a figure they both accepted. Henrik would ride into Cascade and make arrangements at the bank.

"And I'd like you to keep the cow and calf," Benjamin said. "Looks like you've got need of them."

As the men were shaking hands, Henrik's wife appeared at the doorway, a bundle in her arms.

"Hello, Mary," she said. "I thought you might like to see the baby."

"Oh, that would be right nice."

The woman crossed the porch and Mary met her at the rail. Mrs. Bergen lifted the blanket away from the tiny face. The child shifted, eyelids fluttering open, then freed one fist from her wrapping and waved it in the air. Mary reached out a finger and stroked the tiny hand.

"And will you give this to Miss Morgan?" She handed Mary the envelope that Amelia had left with the pie. Mary slipped it into her pocket, noticing that it had not been opened.

Then she spoke to the small girl who'd followed her mother out of the house.

"I got something for you." She reached into her pocket again and pulled out a corn husk doll, wearing a blue calico dress much like the girl's own. "I learned to make these when I was not much bigger than you are."

"What do you say?" Mrs. Henrik prodded.

The girl clutched the doll to her chest. "Thank you."

• • •

Benjamin Reynolds left town the next day, having finished his business at the bank, George's sorrel horse trailing behind him. He had come to see Mary before riding out, giving her another chance to ponder how different two brothers could be, much as they might start life the same and look alike.

• • •

August, 1897

A few weeks later, Mary was tending the daisies and larkspur outside her front door when the lumber mill wagon pulled up. Thomas Whitney held the reins in his good hand, the other cradled in his lap. Beside him sat Amelia Morgan, in her blue traveling suit. Jess barked and ran toward her.

Amelia climbed down and ran both hands over the dog's big head. "You silly old dog. I'm going to miss you."

Mary straightened, fingers working on her hip. "Where you off to?"

"Thomas is taking me to meet the stage to Helena. From there, I'll be going to Dillon, to the new state teacher's college. They're offering a two-year course. When I'm finished, I'll be fully qualified to teach at the elementary level."

Mary gazed thoughtfully at the young man waiting in the wagon, then turned back to Amelia.

"You sure that's what you want to do?"

"Oh, yes. I've always known, really, but I let myself become persuaded that it wasn't possible. Thanks to you and the sisters, and the children at the Mission, I've come to understand that's not true." She gave Mary the same warm smile she'd given her that first day in Cascade. It was different, though, after a season in Montana.

"At least for now," Amelia continued. "Funny, isn't it? I came out here expecting one thing and found another."

"Happen that way," Mary said. "I reckon plenty of folks would say the same." She sure would.

Amelia nodded and held out a small white envelope. "Would you mail this for me, please?"

Mary took the envelope and glanced at the address. *Albert Morgan*, it read, in Pennsylvania. A letter to her father. Good. Good.

"We have something for you." Amelia stepped to the rear of the wagon, where Thomas stood waiting.

A dented old wash tin, barely big enough to hold the rose, heavy with blooms. Small blossoms, their pink-and-white-striped petals soft and sweet-smelling.

Mary blinked once, and then again. *Fool old woman,* she told herself. Crying over a rose.

"Must be the wind," she said as she brushed her cheek. "Blowing something in my eye."

• • •

December 1914, Cascade Courier

The town of Cascade has lost one of its most treasured residents, Mary Fields.

This past week, Mary was found lying in the blowing snow in a field at the edge of town, her dog at her side. The discovery was made by Tommy and Albert Whitney, ages 12 and 10, sons of Thomas and

Amelia Whitney of Cascade. The boys braved fierce winds to summon help. Townsmen carried Mary, senseless with fever, back to her house. She was later taken to Columbus Hospital in Great Falls, where she died.

Mary Fields was born in Tennessee in 1832. She later worked as a chambermaid on the steamship *Robert E. Lee*, plying the waters of the great Mississippi River, where she met Circuit Judge Edmund Dunne and went to work in his family home in Akron, Ohio. There, she met the judge's sister, Mother Amadeus Dunne of the Ursuline Sisters of Toledo, who is well known to the townspeople of Cascade and residents of the surrounding area, despite her departure for Alaska in 1905, where she continues her missionary work among the natives.

Mary came to Montana in 1885 and worked for the Ursuline Sisters at St. Peter's Mission. She moved to Cascade in 1894, where she ran a restaurant. In 1895, she was appointed the Star Route driver, a post she carried out faithfully until retiring in 1903. Mary then ran a laundry service from her home and watched over local children, using her own money to give her young charges fruit and candy.

Mary was well-known for throwing a birthday party for herself every year, at which she gave presents to local children.

As word of Mary's passing spread, townspeople eased their grief by sharing stories. Some recalled that Mary had helped the sisters stay alive in the early years by hunting, trapping, and fishing, and growing a large garden. Others remembered how she fought off a wolf when she and her horses were stranded overnight in a blizzard. Still others told about her fights with men and her soft spot for children. Everyone agreed that there had never been anyone quite like her in Cascade, and never would be.

A service will be held at the new Pastime Theatre, the largest building in town.

Mary Fields loved flowers, baseball, and children, and sitting on the banks of the Missouri River with her dog, smoking a pipe. At her death on December 5, 1914, she was 82 years old.

Historical Notes and Acknowledgments

Writing fiction featuring a historical figure is challenging. Though literate, Mary Fields left no written record and the facts known about her are as sparse as the legends are large. For a novelist, that's both an opportunity and a challenge. Many popular press accounts repeat the same colorful stories, many untrue or exaggerated. "A Bitter Wind," the novella that closes the collection, touches on a few of those myths, and the epilogue summarizes much of what is known about her life.

I chose to write about Mary because her story brings together three fascinating aspects of the nineteenth-century American West that deserve more telling: the story of the formerly enslaved who migrated West after the Civil War, the missionary era, and the woman on her own. While we know little about Mary's early life, all accounts agree that when she came to Montana Territory in 1885, she was propelled by her love and concern for Mother Amadeus. That she stayed until her death in 1914 suggests that the life she found—the life she created—here offered her a sense of freedom and independence she could not get elsewhere, along with a sense of community.

I want you to know these people and the stories they might tell. But I am not the only conduit, and I welcome other storytellers.

Myth is a complicated subject, one I'm not competent to explore except to note that it has always played a huge role in our concept of the West, its history, land, and people. One recent book probing the continuing tensions resulting from myth is *True West: Myth and Mending on the Far Side of America*, by Betsy Gaines Quammen (2023). The stories told in movies, television shows, paintings, and yes, novels, often distort the truth. Paradoxically, they highlight the heroes and successes, along with the violence and conflict. They overlook conquest, along with the failures, such as the homesteaders who gave up and the miners who went bust, the misfits not easily categorized, and the ordinary aspects of daily life. Myth grows from perception, and often from bias. Many of the myths about the West have created an underlying sense of dominion and superiority that has had devastating effects, and which continues to influence life in the West today. We need, as novelist Debra Magpie Earling says, to ask questions about our mythologies.

To some, it might seem contradictory to explore history through fiction, but I believe that by bringing history to life, fiction forces us to question what we think we know about a time and place. About what happened, who was there, and what life was truly like. About humanity, in all its beauty and flaws. Fiction, and especially historical fiction, can tell truths beyond those found in bare facts by exploring possibilities. Stories develop empathy. Understanding. Connection. Compassion. All this not only makes the world more interesting; it inspires us to make it a better place to live.

I am a novelist, not a historian, although I did my best to track down the necessary details; I hope my long career as a lawyer helped with that. I've tried hard to not imagine "facts" about Mary, particularly before she came to Montana, that were not reasonably clear from the record. Writing historical fiction requires filling in gaps and making choices when contrary stories appear. As one example, most accounts say Mary smoked cigars; others say a pipe. I gave her both, liking the visual of the pipe and thinking loose tobacco might have been easier to come by.

I do want to counter some of the tales told about Mary,

Historical Notes and Acknowledgments

still circulating online and elsewhere. Historian Dee Garceau-Hagen says that what is emphasized reveals more about the authors' agendas than about Mary herself, and that is likely true. Legends arose during her lifetime, amplified after her death, and in many ways mirror the mythmaking of the West, which emphasized masculinity, individualism, and violence, as well as the dehumanizing, racist imagery that emerged as the promise of Reconstruction ended.

It's often said that Mary was six feet tall, weighed two hundred pounds, and wore men's clothing. Photographs show a broad woman, perhaps taller than many women of the era; a photo of Mary with the Cascade baseball team shows she was taller than some men, shorter than others. The photos show her wearing a skirt, although she often appears in a jacket or coat that could easily have been made for a man—given her size, her work, and the weather she faced, that was a wise choice. Other tales claim she regularly got in fights with men, punched one who didn't pay for his meal, and shot a man, resulting in her eviction from the Mission. The annals of July 27, 1894, quoted in *Lady Blackrobes: Missionaries in the Heart of Indian Country*, by Irene Mahoney, O.S.U. (2006), report that:

> "The bishop has ordered that [Mary] be dismissed from the Mission but the community has determined to support her wherever she goes. . . . [The bishop] has heard aspersions of the poor woman's character which no one has ever yet been able to prove. She was overbearing and troublesome and yet it was our firm intention to keep her till death."

Sources suggest that the last straw was an argument

between Mary and a neighboring ranch foreman, possibly over a harness, while others say it was a dispute with a white hired hand who claimed Mary was unfairly paid more than he was; no shots were fired. Regardless, the crafty mother superior subverted the bishop's intent that the sisters have no more contact with Mary by helping her get the postal route, bringing her to the Mission regularly.

As a friend said, when I pointed out some of the inaccuracies in an article she'd read about Mary, "it's as if she wasn't amazing enough, all by herself."

One historian has attempted to trace Mary's enslavement to the family of another Ursuline sister, in West Virginia, with results I found unconvincing. Another online article claims Mother Amadeus Dunne's family enslaved Mary, possibly because of the presence of a family named Dunn—note the different spelling—in Hickman County, Tennessee, where some accounts say Mary was born. The Ursulines deny it, and the theory is not consistent with other known facts about the Dunnes. I don't think we will ever know Mary's life before 1870 with any certainty. The 1910 census record notes that Mary and her father were both born in Tennessee, information that most likely came from Mary herself. She chose to celebrate her birthday as March 15, 1832, but acknowledged not knowing the exact date or year. I don't think we will ever know Mary's life before 1870 with any certainty, although scholarship is constantly changing and it's possible that new information will surface to help future researchers fill in some of the gaps.

Novelist Rachel Kadish writes that "Historical fiction, undertaken with integrity, is an act of repair." I hope my stories have done a little of that.

A few notes about other figures on these pages: Mother Amadeus Dunne was born Sarah Theresa Dunne in 1846 in

Akron, Ohio, and died in 1919 in Seattle. An older sister named Sarah had died in infancy, and the family called this daughter Theresa. She joined the Ursulines in Toledo in 1862, taking final vows in 1864, and became Mother Superior in 1874. She came to Montana Territory in 1884 at the request of the Jesuits to establish schools for Indian girls, although the nuns also taught white settlers' children. In that first year, she established schools in Miles City and at St. Labré in southeastern Montana, both now run by the Diocese of Great Falls–Billings, and at St. Peter's; she and the Ursulines also established or took over schools at six other Jesuit missions in Montana, one of which the diocese still runs, and in Alaska. The influence of the Jesuits' and Ursulines' presence continues, as does the investigation and impact into abuses of Indian children, both at schools run by churches and those run by the government. There is no doubting, though, Amadeus's devotion to God and the mission cause, her administrative skills, and the deep affection between her and Mary.

A third historical figure mentioned briefly is Charles M. Russell, the great Western artist. Born in St. Louis in 1864, Russell moved to Montana as a teenager, working as a cowboy and teaching himself to draw, paint, and sculpt. He lived in Cascade for several years, where he kept a studio and married Nancy Cooper before moving to Great Falls in 1897. That same year, he created a pen and ink drawing, "A Quiet Day in Cascade," portraying townspeople coming and going. Fields is shown sitting on the ground after being knocked over by a hog, her basket of eggs upended. Reports are that she was not amused and insisted the episode never happened. According to historian Ellen Baumler, Russell claimed the drawing was a composite of events that occurred at different times. Who knows? Both were larger-than-life characters who lived the myths of the West, and many live on in his work. I highly recommend a visit to the C.M. Russell Museum, home, and studio in Great Falls, and the documentary *Charlie Russell's Old West*, created by Montana PBS.

According to historian and Jesuit priest Wilfred P. Schoenberg, writing in *Montana: The Magazine of Western History* in 1961, the Jesuits left St. Peter's in 1897, nearly forty years after its founding and multiple relocations, because of changes in federal policy toward Indian education. Contract schools like St. Peter's were eliminated in favor of government-run boarding schools, like the one that opened in the former army fort at Fort Shaw in 1892. Loss of the nine-dollar monthly fee for each child was just too much. The Ursulines chose to carry on; this was their western Motherhouse, and home of a successful school for white girls.

Of the Mission itself, little remains. A fire in 1908 destroyed the Jesuits' residence and boys' school. In 1912, the Ursulines finally bowed to the bishop's request that they leave the Mission, their original purpose in coming to Montana, and move into Great Falls, where they established the Ursuline Academy. Some girls' education continued at St. Peter's until a fire in 1918 led to complete closure. The only intact building is the original church, a few piles of burned stones nearby. A rancher's barn sits on the stone foundation of Mount Angela. When I walked the cemetery, it was dotted with gravestones and small monuments for nearby families, and crosses without names that may mark the graves of children who died at the Mission.

According to *Montana Place Names* (Montana Historical Society Press, 2009), the town of Cascade was originally called Dodge, but changed its name in 1887 in hopes of winning the county seat of the new Cascade County. It lost,

Historical Notes and Acknowledgments

but kept the name. Not being the county seat, it would not have had a sheriff or jail. I've given it both, for story purposes. The post office and general store changed locations several times between 1885 and 1897, and the town's saloons changed as well; I've chosen one name and location for each and kept it.

The story of Sister Elizabeth in "Coming Clean" was sparked by the account in *Lady Blackrobes* of a nun who came West with Amadeus in 1884 and remained at St. Labré when Amadeus went to St. Peter's; she left the Mission with a local man and married him. Excerpts from letters between Amadeus and the bishop show that Amadeus was crushed, and blamed herself.

All other characters are figments of my imagination.

Thanks to the Montana Historical Society for allowing me access to their archives, and to reference historian Zoe Ann Stoltz (now retired) and museum manager Jennifer Bottomly O'Looney for answering my questions. Of course, I made the mistakes all by myself.

In addition to the sources mentioned, I consulted many others. A list of references and suggestions for further reading and viewing is on my website. Thanks to Debbie Burke, my longtime critique partner, for her comments on "A Bitter Wind." The late Ramona DeFelice Long, an extraordinary editor and reader, offered invaluable insight for the three short stories, which were originally published in *Alfred Hitchcock Mystery Magazine*, in slightly different form; my thanks to *AHMM* editor Linda Landrigan. Special thanks to the readers who loved those stories and asked for more.

Awards and nominations are a great boost for the writer's sometimes shaky confidence, and I deeply appreciate the Malice Domestic Mystery Convention for awarding "All God's Sparrows" the 2018 Agatha Award for Best Short

Story; Mystery Readers International for honoring "Sparrows" with a 2018 Macavity Award nomination for Best Short Story; the Short Mystery Fiction Society for nominating "Miss Starr's Good-bye" for the 2020 Derringer Award for Best Long Story; and the Western Writers of America for naming "Coming Clean" a 2021 finalist for the Spur Award for Best Short Fiction.

Thanks also to the authors who read and commented on the all-but-finished manuscript, including Edith Maxwell, Ann Parker, Kathleen Grissom, Clare Broyles, Art Taylor, Mark Hummel Leichliter, Sidney Thompson, Chris LaTray, and Quintard Taylor.

My thanks to Bill Harris of Beyond the Page and his team for believing in this project and bringing it to the page, and to cover artist Dar Albert.

The subconscious plays a huge part in the writer's work. One of my most astonishing experiences as a writer came early in writing "A Bitter Wind." A dream focused my mind on a then-nebulous character of a picture bride and gave me the image of a rose carried West in a coffee can, a story I'd heard years earlier, passed down in a friend's family. That same dream pointed me to the work of Montana artist Amy Brakeman Livezey, whose collage style I have long admired, and which influenced the cover. Thanks to FOR Fine Art in Whitefish and Bigfork, Montana, and the Hockaday Museum of Art in Kalispell, Montana, for introducing me to her work.

Finally, my thanks to my husband, Dr. Don Beans, for his willingness to drive down dusty roads, explore old cemeteries, poke our noses into boarded-up buildings, and tour countless museums of art and history. Sharing a passion for our beloved home state has made my life immensely richer.

Readers, it's a treat to hear from you. Drop me a line at Leslie@LeslieBudewitz.com, connect with me on Facebook at LeslieBudewitzAuthor, or join my seasonal mailing list for books news, free short stories, and more. (Sign up on my website, www.LeslieBudewitz.com.) Reader reviews and recommendations are a big boost to authors; if you've enjoyed my books, please tell your friends, in person and online. A book is but marks on paper until you read these pages and make the story yours.

Thank you.

About the Author

Leslie Budewitz is passionate about food, great mysteries, and the Northwest, the setting for her national-bestselling Spice Shop Mysteries and Food Lovers' Village Mysteries, and for her historical fiction. As Alicia Beckman, she writes moody suspense set in the Northwest.

Leslie is a three-time Agatha Award winner: 2011 Best Nonfiction for *Books, Crooks & Counselors: How to Write Accurately About Criminal Law and Courtroom Procedure* (Linden/Quill Driver Books), 2013 Best First Novel for *Death al Dente* (Berkley Prime Crime), first in the Food Lovers' Village Mysteries, and 2018 Best Short Story for "All God's Sparrows" (*Alfred Hitchcock Mystery Magazine*). Her books and stories have also won or been nominated for Derringer, Anthony, Macavity, and Spur awards. A lawyer by trade, she has served as president of Sisters in Crime and on the board of Mystery Writers of America.

Leslie loves to cook, eat, hike, travel, garden, and paint—not necessarily in that order. She lives in Northwest Montana with her husband, Don Beans, a musician and doctor of natural medicine, and their gray tuxedo cat, whose hobbies include napping and eyeing the snowshoe hares who live in the meadow behind the family home.

Visit her online at www.LeslieBudewitz.com, where you'll find maps, recipes, discussion questions, links to her short stories, and more.

Made in the USA
Middletown, DE
24 March 2025

73179252R00099